W9-BMQ-442

GAMBLER'S ODDS

OTHER FIVE STAR WESTERNS BY T. T. FLYNN:

GAMBLER'S ODDS

A WESTERN QUARTET

T. T. FLYNN

FIVE STAR
A part of Gale, Cengage Learning

GALE
CENGAGE Learning®

Farmington Hills, Mich • San Francisco • New York • Waterville, Maine
Meriden, Conn • Mason, Ohio • Chicago

GALE
CENGAGE Learning®

Copyright © 2014 by Thomas B. Flynn, M.D.
The Additional Copyright Information on page 5 constitutes an extension of the copyright page.
Five Star™ Publishing, a part of Cengage Learning, Inc.

ALL RIGHTS RESERVED.
This novel is a work of fiction. Names, characters, places and incidents are either the product of the author's imagination, or, if real, used fictitiously.

No part of this work covered by the copyright herein may be reproduced, transmitted, stored, or used in any form or by any means graphic, electronic, or mechanical, including but not limited to photocopying, recording, scanning, digitizing, taping, Web distribution, information networks, or information storage and retrieval systems, except as permitted under Section 107 or 108 of the 1976 United States Copyright Act, without the prior written permission of the publisher.

The publisher bears no responsibility for the quality of information provided through author or third-party Web sites and does not have any control over, nor assume any responsibility for, information contained in these sites. Providing these sites should not be construed as an endorsement or approval by the publisher of these organizations or of the positions they may take on various issues.

LIBRARY OF CONGRESS CATALOGING-IN-PUBLICATION DATA

Flynn, T. T.
    [Short stories. Selections]
    Gambler's odds : a western quartet / T. T. Flynn. — First edition.
        pages ; cm
        ISBN 978-1-4328-2844-8 (hardcover) — ISBN 1-4328-2844-4 (hardcover)
        I. Title.
    PS3556.L93A6 2015
    813'.54—dc23   2014041382

First Edition. First Printing: April 2015
Published in conjunction with Golden West Literary Agency.
Find us on Facebook– https://www.facebook.com/FiveStarCengage
Visit our website– http://www.gale.cengage.com/fivestar/
Contact Five Star™ Publishing at FiveStar@cengage.com

Printed in the United States of America
1 2 3 4 5 6 7 19 18 17 16 15

ADDITIONAL COPYRIGHT INFORMATION

"Who'll Tame the Wild Tabors?" first appeared in *Star Western* (9/48). Copyright © 1948 by Popular Publications, Inc. Copyright © renewed 1976 by Thomas Theodore Flynn, Jr. Copyright © 2014 by Thomas B. Flynn, M.D., for restored material.

"Brand of the Hangtown Kid" first appeared in *Fifteen Western Tales* (9/45). Copyright © 1945 by Popular Publications, Inc. Copyright © renewed 1973 by Thomas Theodore Flynn, Jr. Copyright © 2014 by Thomas B. Flynn, M.D., for restored material.

"The Quickest Draw" first appeared in Street & Smith's *Western Story Magazine* (12/10/38). Copyright © 1938 by Street and Smith Publications, Inc. Copyright © renewed 1966 by Thomas Theodore Flynn, Jr. Copyright © 1997 by Thomas B. Flynn, M.D., for restored material.

"Ride the Blood Trail" first appeared in *Fifteen Western Tales* (1/49). Copyright © 1948 by Popular Publications, Inc. Copyright © renewed 1976 by Thomas Theodore Flynn, Jr. Copyright © 2014 by Thomas B. Flynn, M.D., for restored material.

CONTENTS

★ ★ ★ ★ ★

Who'll Tame the
Wild Tabors?

★ ★ ★ ★ ★

T.T. Flynn titled this story "Showdown in Blood" and finished it on January 7, 1948. Marguerite E. Harper, his agent, submitted it to Mike Tilden at Popular Publications and this editor bought it on January 19, 1948, paying the author $454. The title was changed to what it is above when it appeared in *Star Western* (9/48) and that title has been retained for its first appearance in book form.

I

The sudden burst of gunfire off the road cut down a running wheel horse in the stage harness. The driver yelled and braked hard. The stage stopped suddenly and the copper-haired girl who had leaned forward to look out was catapulted forward into Brad Tabor.

Brad's arms instinctively closed about her. The slim tautness of her body came lithely and quickly against him. She stayed that way. Her voice had a husky urgency at his cheek. "Have you got a gun?"

"No, ma'am," Brad said.

She had a clean, fresh smell with a heady touch of cologne water. That, Brad thought wryly as she pushed away, was something to be thinking about in a stage hold-up. But then he'd been thinking about her all morning.

"I have one loaded in my handbag," she said intensely.

"Keep it there, ma'am," Brad said, a little sharper than he meant to be. "We'll do better to sit quietly."

The fat drummer sitting next to him had overheard. The drummer blurted angrily: "Young woman, do you want to get me killed?"

She sank back on the opposite seat, beside the two over-dressed, heavily made-up girls. Her reply to the drummer had a kind of scornful accusation.

"Why not? You're not much good when needed, are you?"

Brad thought: *My God, what a spitfire. A wildcat.*

11

He was smiling at the thought when the inevitable bandanna-masked man jerked open the right-hand door and called in gruffly: "Sit quiet, folks! We ain't after trinkets."

The gunman wore overalls and an old canvas brush jacket. His black flat-crowned hat was pulled forward and his hands were in gauntlet gloves despite the heat.

Brad looked twice at the gloves. They were standard issue from some Army quartermaster store, well worn now. The big Colt gun tipped up and covered him. "Who you starin' at? Think we've met before?"

"I doubt it," Brad said politely. "I'm in from California, and not likely to have had the pleasure."

"Well la-de-da an' thank you, ma'am. Ain't you the polite gent. Come to git lathers of money outta the new mines, I'll bet. You a gambler?"

There seemed to be three of them outside the stage. They had been behind green junipers where the road wound through low foothills. Their horses were back somewhere in the brush out of sight.

The driver had not made a sound after his yell. He was quiet when one of the men climbed hurriedly to the high seat, cursed the unsteady horses, and locked the brakes.

Brad answered the gunman at the open door. "I'm not a gambler."

"You'd make a good 'un. Got the fancy look. Anyway, I think you're lyin'."

"Your privilege, with that gun," Brad said politely.

"Think you could do better with one like it?"

Brad smiled slightly and waited.

The man said: "I've seen you some'eres before. Wasn't in Californy. What's your name?"

"Brad Tabor."

The girl had been eyeing him with flushed scorn. His name

seemed a surprise. Her mouth opened as if she meant to speak. Then closed quickly, firmly. She sat stiffly beside the dance-hall girls, and now she seemed to be studying him.

The gunman said—"Tabor!"—explosively behind the bandanna mask. Then he laughed. "I'll be damned. All the way from Californy, huh?"

"Correct," Brad said.

The other two gunmen were at the boot. There was a heavy thud in the road. "Got it!" a voice called. "Let's get goin'!"

It was over like that . . . shots, talk, and then they were alone. Brad stepped out of the stage while departing voices were still audible back in the juniper brush. He faced back to the step, protesting, as the copper-headed girl started out after him. "You'd best not, ma'am."

She came anyway. Brad had to help her down. She came off the steps lightly as a boy, not speaking, and she stood at the road edge as Brad mounted to the driver's seat.

The raw-boned driver had slipped down in a huddle on the footboard, one arm hanging limply over. He had been shot through the head. He had probably been dying as he yelled and braked hard.

The girl was wiping her eyes when Brad called for the fat drummer to get out and help him.

"I thought we'd find something like this," Brad said, looking down at her. "You should have listened to me and stayed inside. Is he a friend of yours?"

"He's Jed Simmons," the girl said, not trying to hide her tears. "He was lazy and no-good, mean and worthless . . . but his wife loved him. I'm thinking about her." Brad nodded, liking her for that, and then she said: "There were only three of them. You could have killed at least two if you knew how to point a gun."

"What about the third one, ma'am?" Brad asked her. "Or

13

others who might have been out there?"

Her quick gesture was scornful. "Go back to California, Brad
Tabor, if you worry about such things. You won't last on
Candlestick. Not now."

Brad eyed her with new interest. The sun stirred living copper
tints in her hair and found freckles on the bridge of her small
nose. She was younger than he was and he was twenty-four. He
thought again: *Lordy, what a wildcat. California never had one like
her.*

Then he thought of her litheness in his arms, the brush of
her coppery hair at his cheek, the fragrance of her nearness. He
stood without moving, looking at her. The fat drummer's gasp
at the off-wheel brought him around.

"Makes me sick to look at him."

"Help lift him out of there and get sick afterward," Brad told
the man shortly.

The drummer did that, and then walked to the back of the
stage alone. Brad was cutting the dead wheeler horse out of the
harness with his pearl-handled pocket knife when mule-drawn
ore wagons crawled over the rise ahead. The stage was sighted.
Muleskinners, coiling long bull whips, ran forward. They knew
the girl and called her Miss Sally, with a grinning respect that
gave Brad rather a shamed relief. He hadn't really thought it,
but she'd been friendly with the two percentage girls and could
have been traveling with them.

The muleskinners agreed there wasn't much to do now but
get the stage into Piedras and report to the sheriff. The dead
man could ride on top, wrapped in a tarpaulin. Brad said he
would drive, and they accepted it.

A big black-bearded muleskinner spat and said: "So they got
a money box? Bet a turkey's neck it belonged to old King Tabor.
It'll curdle him."

Brad made no comment. The copper-haired girl looked at

him, started to speak, and then did not. A team of wagon mules dragged the dead horse off the road. Brad climbed up and gathered the long reins.

The girl mounted lightly and sat beside him. The big-bearded muleskinner had given her a hand up. He explained to Brad: "Miss Sally knows the road."

Brad shrugged. He let off the brakes and yelled with his swing of the long whip. The tip exploded between the leaders with a pistol report. The horses rushed the stage away amid the approving judgment of the muleskinners.

The stage whirled dust past the strung-out ore wagons and raced over the rise beyond. There was a curving downgrade, another turn at the bottom, and a rough stretch of wash beyond. Brad took the stage down fast, letting it ride the leathers hard. On the next grade he eased the horses and looked over his shoulder at the tarp-covered body.

The girl was sitting beside him with her eyes half closed, swaying easily with the rocking stage. The breeze whipped hair tendrils about her small ears. She had an oddly pleased but unsmiling look of relaxed contentment.

She likes a fast run, Brad thought. *The more you look at her, the prettier she gets.* Then he asked a blunt question. "How did you know I was going to Candlestick?"

Without looking at him, she replied: "King Tabor has only one grandson."

"King?" Brad repeated. "King Tabor . . . is that what they call him, instead of Kingsley Tabor?"

She nodded.

"King Tabor," Brad mused. He thought it over. "King of Candlestick, ma'am . . . or of Piedras Range?"

She sat in silence, still not looking at him. When her head did turn slowly, she was unsmiling, indifferent. "You're his kin. You should know."

"I haven't seen him since I can remember." Brad grinned at her. "I don't know your name."

"Sarah Williams."

"I like Sally better."

She had looked back at the trotting horses and the road ahead. The indifference was about her like a cloak, and it came evident in her reply. "Only friends call me Sally."

"I still like it better," Brad said. "Sally Wildcat."

Her flush and look at him were angry.

Brad chuckled and busied himself with driving. They rode side-by-side on the high-rocking seat in silence.

II

The old figure reining the gray horse off the wagon-cluttered main street of Piedras could only be Kingsley Tabor. Brad saw him from the window of the sheriff's office. He watched the erect body in the high-cantled, silver-crusted Mexican saddle. A white broad-brimmed hat was pulled slightly forward over a thin old face that had a mustache like a white bar above tight lips.

"He's coming," Brad said.

Orrie Simms, the sheriff, was another lean old-timer, who seemed to waste few words. Brad had liked him from the first. Simms sat beside a roll-top desk that was stuffed, piled with dusty untouched papers, and said dryly: "Fire in his eye, I'll bet."

King Tabor came in talking coldly. "They say another money box has been taken!" He saw Brad standing near the window and stared. "So you got here?" He turned, speaking to the sheriff again. "I had ten thousand in that box, Orrie."

"That much?" Orrie Simms said. "Who had it slipped on the stage on the sly, and brought on without a shotgun messenger?"

"My idea," King Tabor admitted shortly. "It didn't work.

16

What have you done about it?"

"Sent Bill Janes and a few men to look around. It'll be dark before they can trail five miles. If there's a trail."

"Were any of the thieves recognized?"

"Nope."

King Tabor was like a curt cold stranger standing there, even when he asked: "Brad, would you know any of them again?"

"One man wore old Army gloves," Brad said thoughtfully. "When the fingers of the left hand bent in once, the little finger of that glove stayed out, as if nothing was inside. I could be mistaken."

"He told me about it," Orrie Simms said, getting up. "I can't place a man shy a little finger. I'll ride up to the mines and ask around. Plenty of new ones in and out these days."

"Too many new ones!" King Tabor said with sudden harshness. "This is grass country. Should have stayed that way."

"You started grabbing mines yourself," Simms reminded.

"I had to, when it started," Tabor said impatiently.

"I reckon you thought so," Simms said dryly. "You always did keep a jump ahead of Bo."

King Tabor's thin face hardened. "Never mind Bo Kemstead." He turned. "Brad, there's a horse at the feed barn. The buckboard will take your baggage."

He was still like a stranger, this tall, fine-looking old man talking—proud, cold, distant.

Brad nodded. He saw Orrie Simms studying him with a curious, impersonal thoughtfulness as he went out.

The same curious study came on the hostler's face at the feed barn when Brad said his name was Tabor. The hostler led out a big gray gelding, almost a match for King Tabor's fine horse. He lugged over a saddle that was another match, a high-cantled, hand-tooled, silver-mounted Mexican saddle, like King Tabor's saddle.

Brad looked at it thoughtfully and shook his head. "How about that old one hanging over there? It looks like an easy seat."

"Orders was to put this 'un on your horse, mister."

"The other one," Brad said.

The hostler stood uncertainly. Brad built a cigarette and waited. The man shrugged and cinched on the other saddle. It had been used hard but it was comfortable when Brad swung up.

King Tabor had stopped at the bank. He reined out and met Brad in the street, and said sharply: "I left a good saddle for you."

"I took this one," Brad said. He sensed a cold will hardening at being crossed, and waited.

What Tabor might have replied was shut off by three men, wheeling their horses out from a hitch rack, and the leader reining up by them. The stranger was white-haired and massive. From worn-out black hat turned up in front to patched overall riding pants, he was dressed like a forty-a-month line-camp hand. But there was a huge grinning force about him. It was an unpleasant grin. His question had a sly prod. "You bringing in some help, King?"

"My grandson, Brad Tabor . . . Bo Kemstead."

"Ladder P brand, if you ain't heard," Bo Kemstead said.

"I've heard," Brad said.

"Bet you have." Bo Kemstead chuckled. He indicated the two riders flanking him. "My nephew, Jip Haines. The redtop is Steve Williams, another nephew." Dust jumped from the worn overall cloth as Bo Kemstead slapped a big thigh in gusty humor. "My kinfolks're squatting close, waiting for old Bo to cash in. You only got one, King." Bo Kemstead turned his head and spat. The sly prod in his voice became stronger. "He's got a likeness to you, King. But I'd say he favors his pappy more.

18

How about it? Think this one'll stay?"

Brad's glance swung to King Tabor. The white bar mustache lay across stone calm. "Perhaps," King Tabor said briefly. He shook out the reins and rode on. Or, Brad guessed as he rode, too, with a lift of his hand to the three men, it could be repressed fury in his grandfather.

"I heard about the hold-up!" Kemstead called. His booming voice carried along the street. "If it's shorted you, King, I can lend some cash!"

"It hasn't," King Tabor replied, riding on.

Brad had the deep queer feeling all this had happened to him before. All of it. Bo Kemstead's wheeling out to talk. This pine-straight old man, riding coldly, in the silver-mounted saddle. All of it, including this same street in Piedras town, and men watching them ride slowly by, studying them. The feeling was strong and Brad knew why. It had happened like this to his easy, kindly father, now dead many years. To King Tabor and his son. Now the tall old man was white-haired. He was King Tabor—riding with his grandson. But nothing had changed. Nothing. Brad's mouth tightened and coldness came into his own eyes.

New buildings were going up in Piedras. Saloons, dance halls, stores were spreading out along the wheel-cut main street. Adobe, log, and even a few frame houses were being built beyond the older ones. Orrie Simms had explained that the mines were in the mountains to the east, scattered up several cañons. All new mines, none large as yet. But new men were drifting in fast and Piedras, the supply and shipping point, was booming. One could see it. Hard-boot miners and prospectors were on the walks. Well-dressed men carrying the smooth stamp of city streets moved about. Big freight and ore wagons, buggies, buckboards, saddle horses, and pack mules stood on the streets, and moved in and out of town, lifting dust.

"Not like it was when you first saw it," Brad mused to the

straight old man he sided.

They were at the edge of town. Tabor's gesture went to snow peaks tipping the horizon in the far north. "Grass was belly-high on a horse then, from the Chasucos in the north there, to Apache Flat, fifty miles southwest. The longhorns I brought up from the Texas brush had never seen anything like it." He rode for a moment, thinking, shoulders back. "Neither had I," he said. "Grass, water, land, and Apaches."

Brad waited, knowing it from his father, who had gotten it from this cold, straight old man long ago. He wanted to hear it again.

King Tabor seemed to say it aloud to himself, reaching far back into memory. "Only a few of us were in here then. Mostly young. Younger than you are. Apaches came down and we fought them. Rustlers moved in and we shot them. A few of us lasted out drought. We took Piedras range and we held it." He paused again, looking into the distance. "The soft ones moved out," he said harshly.

Brad said nothing.

King Tabor turned his head. "You've had some experience in the California mines, which is why I sent for you. In the next day or so we'll see some of Candlestick and the lay of the country." He faced ahead and finished evenly: "Then we'll see how soft you are."

Brad held his silence. They rode on side-by-side, like two strangers who had fallen in together for a time. . . .

Brad had heard about the ranch house, too. Adobe walls three feet thick, the rooms built around an inside patio and a deep-dug well. It was a fort and had been used as a fort, and it had not changed.

Nothing much, Brad found in the next few days, had changed since King Tabor's son and young bride had left Candlestick and Piedras range for good. They had gone to California and had stayed.

Candlestick and Ladder P still dominated the range. Men still were friendly with Candlestick or with Ladder P, or they kept aloof. It had been so since young Bo Kemstead and young Kingsley Tabor had reached Piedras grass in the same summer, long ago. The first time they met they had fought each other to a standstill with bare fists, and had ridden away without shaking hands.

Later, the girl they both courted had married Kingsley Tabor. Bo Kemstead had never married, never forgiven that. Candlestick and Ladder P had put up the first line fence on the range, with armed guards patrolling. They had disputed water holes and range rights, fences, mavericks, strayed cattle. Now and then like lobo wolves against common prey they had thrown in together against rustlers.

The winter of the long blizzard King Tabor had cut his own fences and let starving Ladder P cattle in to stacked wild hay on Candlestick land. Then Tabor had damned the good deed by sending word to Bo Kemstead that Candlestick would feed even a hungry dog. Bo Kemstead had led his men across ice-encrusted snow, and had driven his staggering steers back and shot them out of their misery on his own land.

It had been that way since the beginning, since that summer when long, lean, headstrong young Kingsley Tabor had led the spooked remnants of his longhorn herd out of the far *brazado* thickets of deep Texas. It had started when Big Bo Kemstead, his hair in those days a wild reddish mane, his deep voice bawling in anger or humor, had brought his down-at-the-heels outfit of trail-gaunted riders and cattle to the tall Piedras grass. Bo Kemstead was afraid of nothing that walked or crawled, man, beast, Apache—or Kingsley Tabor.

King Tabor had run more cattle, fenced more grass when the

time came, made more money. Bo Kemstead had challenged him every step of the way. It had made Bo unrelenting. It had turned Kingsley Tabor cold, hard, unyielding.

All that Brad knew. His mother had told him. She had lived unhappily on Candlestick as a young bride and had left and gone back to California. Her young husband had followed her. They had stayed and had been happy. Tabor had never written them until notified his son had died. Then, once a year, he had written briefly, coldly, as if reluctantly keeping contact. He was King Tabor now, old, hard, unyielding—and alone.

There was a hardness about Candlestick riders, too. They were picked for that, Brad guessed. Shaffer, the foreman, had cold eyes and a hard mouth. The rest of his men were no better. They kept a taciturn reserve when King Tabor was near. But they all had one thing in common. They were straight-riding, gun-wearing, hard-eyed men who had no use for weakness. They were not always taciturn. Brad was with them a time or two when there was grinning and joshing. Some of it included him a time or two. But they were Tabor men, and King Tabor's mark was on Candlestick and everyone close to him.

When Brad rode out with the tall old man, the two of them remained like strangers, even when Tabor talked of the ranch and the new mines. He spoke only brief facts, saying nothing personal. The reserve was there the morning he had handed Brad a gun belt and holstered gun, and said: "We'll ride to Piedras and the mines today. Can you shoot?"

"A little," Brad said.

He looked at the silver-handled .44, thumbed the cylinder, tried the drop. It was a fine gun. Tabor had only the best of everything. Brad put the gun back in the holster and returned the belt.

"Brought my own gun," he said briefly, and went to his room and came back, buckling on the belt. It was supple and soft with age, and sagged comfortably, the holster low and a little forward.

King Tabor looked hard at the worn, cedar-handled gun, and reached for it and examined it. His mouth tightened under the bar of white mustache. He handed it back. His comment was harsher than usual. "I gave it to your father. He was too much of a weakling to use it."

Brad was tart and lean, too. His level look rested equally on the older man's face, tightening, hardening as he holstered the old gun and said: "I'm ready."

They rode toward Piedras like strangers. When Tabor finally broke the silence, he did not turn his head. His voice was flat, even. He said: "I'm almost broke." He rode long seconds, waiting for answer, and then his voice came stronger. "I said I'm almost broke!"

Brad nodded. "I thought so."

They rode a far distance toward Piedras. The rising sun was lifting heat shimmer over the sweeping range. A thread of yellow dust on the horizon marked the Piedras road. The dark upthrust of the mountains seemed not far beyond. From those forested slopes, out of those dark cañons breech-clouted Apaches had come down on men who had dug in on the long grass to stay, and had stayed.

"How did you know Candlestick was broke?" Tabor asked, finally breaking their silence.

"Five cars of Candlestick steers took the sidetrack at Three Wells while I waited for the Piedras stage. They weren't prime. They were being shipped out of season. There's grass and water on Candlestick."

"True," Tabor said.

"The bunkhouse is half empty. You've laid off hands. Something happened in the bank the other day you didn't like. One of the gunmen who held up the stage laughed when he heard my name. If you're broke," Brad went on evenly, "I'd guess a few suspect it. You can't be king of the range and not be watched."

King Tabor rode, staring ahead. His face was bloodless, stone-hard.

Brad filled in the rest of it. "Bo Kemstead would be first to know and spread it around. He's waited a long time, hasn't he?"

"Too long!" King Tabor said. "Bo couldn't wait any longer. He's getting old." Tabor's voice began to shake. His face flushed. "It's turned him into a thief, a rustler, and a killer. It's made him into a lying snake fit to be shot on sight. I should have killed him forty years ago, instead of letting him grow old and collect his worthless kinfolks around him to tear the belly out of Candlestick like yellow dogs."

Brad listened, his own face hard. "That's why you sent for me?"

"You're my son's son. The only kin left. The last Tabor. You'll have Candlestick someday. Your father was a weakling. He left me alone. I've prayed you were the man I thought your father would be. Now we'll see. I know what has to be done. Together we'll do it."

Brad said slowly: "You've hated Kemstead a lifetime. It's poisoned you and everything you touched. It drove your son away and he was a better man than you. He could shoot better and fight better. I've seen him do it. But he wouldn't hold a grudge. He didn't like to hate. You've nursed hate alone and you can play it out alone. I didn't come from California to pick up your grudge against Kemstead."

"What brought you?"

"We're the last two Tabors and you sent for me. I wanted a welcome and I got poison. The same poison that drove your son and his wife away. It's driven you like a bull-whipped mule. It's made you King Tabor, with nobody caring what happens to you."

The harsh voice said: "Is that all?"

"Not all," said Brad. "I'm your grandson. If I'd found you sick, I'd have tended you. If you'd been hungry, I'd have rustled your grub. If you'd reached for my hand and said . . . 'Howdy, welcome.' . . . I'd have thought I was coming home. But all you wanted was another Tabor to hate Bo Kemstead." Brad made a hard gesture of refusal. "My father walked away from it. Play your grudge out alone."

"That all?"

Brad started a cigarette. "That's all."

"Pack up and travel back where you came from."

Brad reined up silently.

King Tabor rode on without turning his head. The big gray horse and the straight-backed rider grew small in the distance, and the rider did not look back.

Brad sat watching, smoking the cigarette down, until King Tabor was out of sight. He ground out the cigarette against the saddle horn and reined north toward Ladder P.

Bo Kemstead's place was another old fort-like house, a great square low adobe, thick-walled, with huge pine trunks from the mountains holding the thick dirt roof, Spanish style, like Candlestick, with an inner patio and water well. The two houses, Candlestick and Ladder P, might have been built to match each other. And they had.

Brad had heard it from his father. King Tabor had started to build first. Kemstead had built a bigger house but just like it. The girl they had both been courting had gone to live at Candlestick.

Brad had a musing thought as he rode toward the big house. He wondered how it would have been if the girl had married Bo

Kemstead. It brought the first slow smile of the day. Brad Tabor would have been a Kemstead.

He swung off toward an outlying corral where dust and a plunging rider marked a horse being broken. A massive white-haired figure was perched on the top corral rail. The figure turned and sighted him and vaulted to the ground.

A younger man with the same massive look ducked through the gate poles and sided Bo Kemstead.

The rider sawed the blowing horse to a stop and watched. He was another big one, with the long slab-jawed, narrow-eyed look of the nephew called Jip Haines, who Brad had met in Piedras.

Bo Kemstead had the same huge grinning force about him, the same unpleasant smile. "Git lost, young feller?"

"No," Brad said. He sat easy in the saddle, looking about.

Bo Kemstead dressed like a range drifter, but his fences were tight and strong, his big house freshly plastered with adobe, his corrals, outbuildings, windmills a match for anything on Candlestick.

"You're the first Tabor in twenty-five years who's crossed the fence line. Was your pappy that time. Come to pay a friendly call?" he said.

"I've heard," Brad said, smiling a little. "You lined a buffalo gun on him and said the shortest way home was straight out from the sights."

Bo Kemstead pushed his old black hat back and grinned. "I was young and hot-headed then. I'm old and broke-down now, with my kinfolks around me, waiting for the end. Meet a couple more of my nephews. This 'un by me is a Kemstead. Bill Kemstead. That 'un on the horse in another, Haines. Bo Haines they named him, thinking it would please me." Bo Kemstead spat, grinning. "Ain't he a fine one? Knows horses. Did a hitch in the cavalry. A man oughta be proud to have such a fine young feller named after him."

Bo Kemstead's grin broadened as Brad nodded to the nephews and they stared in suspicious silence.

"Step down and visit. You remind me of your pappy before he lit for Californy. We're mighty proud to have you on Ladder P."

"Thanks," Brad said, staying easy in the saddle. His glance drifted over the nephews, over big massive Bill Kemstead, over long-jawed, narrow-eyed Bo Haines. He looked back at the huge, grinning, white-haired old man who his grandfather hated.

"I just stopped by," Brad said mildly, "to ask if you were a thief."

III

"A what?" Bo Kemstead asked explosively.

"A thief," Brad said. "A rustler, a liar, and a killer."

Bo Haines came off the horse fast, running to a gun belt hanging on a corral pole. Bill Kemstead slid a hand toward the holstered six-gun he was wearing.

Bo Kemstead lifted his voice at them. "Keep outta this, you fools! He didn't call me anything. He asked me. I'll tell him!"

Bo Kemstead rubbed short, white stubble on his chin. He grinned. "I've closed my eyes and run my iron on a maverick or two. That makes me a thief. I've met some quick draws and walked away. Makes me a killer, don't it? I come on Piedras grass young and proddy, with my road band on the damnedest passel of tallies you ever seen. We'd swept up every stray on the trail and she was a long trail and I meant to get a start come hell or high water. Makes me a rustler, I reckon." Bo Kemstead rubbed his chin again. "As for being a liar, who ain't now and then?"

The nephew beside him was standing stiffly, watching fixedly. "Bo, he's making a fool outta you."

Bo Kemstead turned his head. "Shut your mouth, Bill. Keep it shut! Now then, Tabor, what trick's the old man figured up, sending you over to prod me this way?"

"No trick," Brad said. "It's a friendly visit. No offense meant with the questions."

Bo Kemstead's mouth snapped trap-hard. "Friendly . . . from Candlestick?"

"I'm from California," Brad said, gathering the reins. "I'm leaving Candlestick. I take a man as I find him. You've been kindly and I thank you kindly."

Silence held the spot as Brad rode away. He was almost out of earshot when he heard Bo Kemstead's savage order. "Shut up! I'm thinking!"

Orrie Simms stood beside his cluttered sheriff's desk and the dry humor was lacking in his blue eyes. "Make you a deputy? Hell, no!" The revolving chair sagged back as Orrie sat down. "If I make a Candlestick man a deputy, I've got to balance with one of Bo Kemstead's men."

"I've left Candlestick," Brad reminded.

"You rode off Candlestick, you didn't leave it. You're a Tabor." Orrie squinted. "Take my advice and light a shuck back to where you came from, young feller."

"I'll take your advice," Brad said. He was wearing the old cedar-handled gun. The sheriff's eyes kept straying to it. Then Orrie Simms's look became intent when Brad asked: "What about the men who shot the stage driver the other day?"

"We run their trail into Apache Flat *malpais,*" Orrie Simms said. "Lost it there. Found the money box empty."

"That ends it?"

"Probably." The lean old sheriff sat unsmiling. Brad stood, watching him. Orrie broke the silence with dry bluntness. "I've been around here a long time. I know when I got a chance to come up with a man. Too many strangers around now. Lose a trail and that's the end of it . . ."—Orrie cleared his throat—"if tracks're all a man has got to go on. Ain't anyone around town or at the mines who's shy a little finger on his left hand. I've looked."

They watched each other in silence again. Brad grinned and turned to the door. "I'll light a shuck back to where I came from."

Orrie Simms nodded and watched silently as Brad walked out and closed the door.

The town had the same look of crowding and activity. There was a Saturday feel in the air, a covert excitement that made each day like pay day. Grass and cattle never made a town like this. It took placer gold or hard-rock ore to put this hustling excitement in the air.

Brad watched it from the saddle along the main street and dismounted in front of a small restaurant. A white-lettered sign bordered in red said *THE GRUB BOX, Miss Sarah Williams, Prop.* Brad walked in and sat at the front end of the counter. Sally Williams was behind it and there were no other customers at the moment.

"Steak, coffee, and apple pie, ma'am," Brad said politely, and then he picked up the glass of water she put out and said— "Sally Wildcat"—and drank gravely.

Sally Williams went on to the kitchen doorway and gave the order to a wrinkled Chinaman standing there.

Brad noticed that the counter, tables, and walls were spotless. So were the dotted window curtains and the neat apron Sally wore. Her copper hair was twisted in a bun at the back of her neck and she was flushed and angry as she returned with bread and butter.

"I didn't think you'd last on Candlestick," Sally said coldly. "If you don't take that gun off, someone will take it away from you before you get on the stage."

"It's an old one, ma'am," he said. "Not worth taking." Brad smiled across the counter. "You get news in here quick."

"Most of it."

Brad stirred sugar in the coffee. "Maybe you've heard who killed the stage driver."

When he looked up, Sally Williams had a strained look. Something like fright retreated into the dark depths of her eyes as he watched.

"I haven't heard," Sally said. She hesitated. "Have you?"

Brad shook his head. "Does your Uncle Bo Kemstead own this place?"

"He does not." She was emphatic.

Brad grinned. "I met your brother Steve the other day. And your cousin Jip Haines. Today I rode over to call on Bo Kemstead, and met your cousin Bill Kemstead and your cousin Bo Haines. And I hear there's cousin Tex Haines and cousin Ike Yancy at the mines . . . cousins everywhere." Brad smiled. "And Bo Kemstead's place big enough for all . . . but I hear you room with the schoolteacher, at the preacher's house, and work hard here in town all alone."

Sally hardly seemed to be listening. The strained look was back on her face. "You rode over to see Uncle Bo? Why?"

"Friendly like. He was neighborly," he said.

She watched his face. Brad thought she suddenly looked tired and worried. Her opinion had a sudden passionate scorn. "Only a fool would ride around like that, wearing a gun he's afraid to use."

Riders cantering by outside drew Brad's look. He sat motionlessly watching Shaffer, the Candlestick foreman, and seven of the Candlestick men go past. They rode closely bunched, straight-backed, not looking to right or left. There was an air of reserved detachment about them, a look of self-sufficiency.

They were King Tabor's men, from Candlestick, and the mark was on them. Brad's look narrowed slightly. They had the usual belt guns. But each man had come to town with a saddle carbine. Sally was looking through the front window, too. Brad watched her profile for a moment.

"Your Uncle Bo was neighborly," he said. "I found it easy to like him."

Sally looked quickly, as if she had forgotten him. "I like Bo Kemstead, too!" she said intensely. "But my name isn't Tabor. I don't belong on Candlestick."

"We could change that," Brad said.

He watched anger rush color to her cheeks, and just then three muleskinners walked in, talking. One red-faced muleskinner with a raspy voice was saying: "Them Candlestick men looked proddy."

The man behind him chuckled. "Maybe they're after Blackie."

Sally Williams knew the wagon men. She ignored Brad until she brought his steak. By then more customers had come in and she was busy. Brad ate leisurely, and then rolled a cigarette. The men at Candlestick had said Sally Williams served the best food in Piedras. He believed it now.

He sat thinking of what he knew and what he didn't know. His mind kept jumping back to Shaffer and the Candlestick riders.

Color had stayed in Sally Williams's cheeks. She was smiling and busy. She traded banter with some of the men along the counter. But a time or two, when her face fell into repose, she looked worried.

Brad was lighting a second cigarette when the door came open before a hard shove. A pockmarked stranger carrying a rifle stepped in fast, big-roweled spurs jingling.

"Bo Kemstead or any of his men in here or in town?" he asked sharply.

Sally Williams replied: "I haven't seen any of them."

Brad took in the stranger's gray dusty hat, long bony face, and long clean-shaven upper lip. He marked the way the man held the rifle ready in the left hand and kept the right hand ready near the belt gun. Dog teeth showed under the stranger's long upper lip as a grin formed. He seemed excited but not worried as he spoke.

"They better get in town. Old man Tabor's hide finally got shot full of lead. Steve Williams and I brought the old goat outta Jericho Cañon in a buckboard. He's a goner if I ever seen one. A bunch of Candlestick riders hung with guns're taking Steve back to the cañon to get a tally on what happened."

Brad was on his feet by then. The stranger had gone a step past him, and caught the movement and wheeled suspiciously.

"Who shot him?" Brad asked.

"Pete Kirkland, who runs the Tabor mines. The spraddle-legged little feller who tallies books says Tabor and Kirkland had an argument and rode up the cañon together. Steve Williams was up near the Kemstead mine and heard a couple shots. He found Tabor by his horse and we brought Tabor to town. Kirkland wasn't around. Looks like he lit out."

"Where's Tabor?" Brad asked.

"Doc Jones's office down the street."

"Sheriff know about it?"

"Yep."

They were all watching as Brad turned and dropped two silver dollars on the counter. The sound brought Sally Williams's look from the stranger to him. All color had left her face. Fright was back in the dark depths of her eyes. She was removing the apron. Her hands were unsteady.

"Don't let your men kill Steve," she said.

"They're not my men," Brad told her.

"Don't say that!" Sally flared. "You're a Tabor. They're your men if King Tabor is dead."

The dog teeth showed in the stranger's watchful grin.

"What's your name?" Brad asked him.

"You got worries now, sonny. Don't bother about me."

Brad nodded and let it stand that way as he went out.

A small crowd had gathered before the doctor's white-painted frame office. Someone must have recognized Brad on the running horse. Men stepped aside as he ducked under the hitch rack and went fast into the front room of the doctor's office. The sick-sweet smell of chloroform came from an inner room as he opened the door.

A gray-haired woman, evidently the doctor's wife, waved him back. Behind her he saw a sheet-covered table under a skylight and the doctor working with rolled-up sleeves.

"I'm Brad Tabor, ma'am. How is he?"

"Dead any minute if fools, including you, interrupt me," the doctor snapped savagely without looking up. "Get out!"

Brad backed out and stood for a moment, staring at the blank door, and then walked outside.

A stranger asked: "How is he?"

"Bad," Brad said.

He sensed something more than curiosity in the small crowd. That straight still figure in there under the doctor's hands was Tabor, of Candlestick. King Tabor. They might not like him, but he was still King Tabor. Brad left his horse at the rack and walked fast toward the bank and he felt the weight of their eyes on his back. He was Brad Tabor.

Carson Murray headed the Piedras bank. Brad found him a heavy, gray-haired man who worked in shirt sleeves. Murray was unsmiling as they shook hands in a small back room of the bank.

"I knew your father," Murray said. "Is Kingsley dead yet?" It was hard to tell how he felt about it.

"Not yet," Brad said, staying on his feet when Murray indicated a chair beside the roll-top desk. "Who owns this bank?"

"The stockholders," Murray said, studying him. "Tabor and Kemstead have been the biggest stockholders. I owned a few shares when the bank opened. Never bought any more."

"What's happened to Candlestick in the last year or so?"

"A cowman tried to be a miner," said Murray laconically. "A man can be smart at one and a fool at the other."

Brad nodded. "How did it happen?"

"Kemstead had been staking a half-witted prospector named Butler to keep the old fellow from starving. Butler wandered around in the mountains for several years. One day he came into town with a sack of high-grade ore from an outcrop he'd uncovered up Jericho Cañon. And that, blew the lid off. Word went out we had a rich strike. The town . . . and most of the ranchmen rushed out to have a try. If a half-wit like old Butler could strike it rich, anyone could."

"I've seen it happen," Brad said. "I'll guess Tabor had to have a mine, too. He bought a claim. Bo Kemstead got another. Tabor went him one better. It takes money to open up hard-rock claims. Tabor bled Candlestick to do it."

"Something like that," Murray agreed. He stood there, not friendly, not unfriendly, studying his visitor.

"Why isn't Bo Kemstead bled out, too?"

Murray said: "Bo didn't have bad luck. Things changed fast around here. Outlaws moved in. Rustling started. They rustled Candlestick harder than any other outfit. You were on the stage when Kingsley lost ten thousand he couldn't afford. He's lost more."

"Why didn't he draw his money through the bank here?"

"Angry," said Murray calmly. "Kingsley had borrowed too much. I shut him off. First time he'd been crossed like that."

"Bo Kemstead backed you on it?"

"I'd have done it anyway," Murray said. "I've run the bank my way. Tabor and Kemstead each knew the other would back me in a showdown, if only to be contrary."

"Bo Kemstead backed you in shutting off Candlestick's credit. Then he offered to lend his own money the other day."

"He'd take security and count on getting Candlestick quicker," Murray said, and shrugged. "Bo knew Kingsley would go broke and starve before he'd borrow a dollar that way."

"Ore is being hauled out. Isn't it paying?"

"Not enough, evidently," Murray said. "Tabor stopped telling me his business. Bo Kemstead is shipping out enough high-grade to almost meet his development costs. So far all the mines are sorting out the best of the high-grade and letting the rest wait until we get a mill in here. Won't be long."

Brad started a cigarette. "Know anything about this Pete Kirkland who shot him?"

"You don't seem to know much, young man."

"Not much," Brad agreed. "I need to now."

"Kirkland seemed a good man. Handy with his fists or a gun, but he had some rough ones working for him. Bo Kemstead went to Denver and hired him. Kirkland had a run-in with Ike Yancy, Bo's oldest nephew, and got fired. Tabor hired him. That was almost a year ago. Things were just getting started. A good man was hard to find."

"Ike Yancy gives orders?"

"He's a mining man. Bo showed hard-headed sense and sent for Ike. He was lucky to have a mining man in the family. It's kept Bo from making mistakes. He's let Yancy pretty well run most of the mines."

"Thanks," Brad said, ready to go.

A gesture stopped him. The gray-haired banker was sober and blunt. "Let me have my say, Tabor. Candlestick and Ladder

P have been powder waiting for the right match since I can remember. This may be the match. I'm told Shaffer and some of his men have taken Steve Williams back to the mines. It sounds bad. If Candlestick and Bo Kemstead go at each other finally, they'll tear this town and this range apart. What will you do about it now?"

"I'll ride over to Jericho Cañon and see what's happening," Brad said. "If you can get word to Bo Kemstead, tell him I still think he seemed neighborly."

"Neighborly!" Carson Murray repeated explosively. When Brad closed the door, the banker was standing there, shaking his head.

The sheriff, Brad heard down the street, was already far on the way to Jericho Cañon with deputies. Brad rode fast that way.

Behind him in Doc Jones's small office, King Tabor clung to life by the thinnest thread. He had been drilled twice and left for dead. But he was King Tabor—too old, hard, cold, and tough to die quickly. Now men were wondering about the next Tabor.

Dust lifted ahead where three freight wagons crawled toward Jericho Cañon. The big muleskinner on the lead wagon had a black ropy beard. He was the one who had helped Sally Williams up to the driver's seat of the stage. He called as Brad reined his blowing horse abreast, "Who you trying to ketch? The sheriff or the Tabor men?"

"How was Steve Williams when he passed here?"

"Looked like he was riding with trouble. His sister figures it's bad."

"Did she ride this way?"

"Killing her horse trying to ketch up. 'Blackie', she says, 'if they kill him, I'll carry a gun against Candlestick meself!' And damned if she won't, mister. There's a gal with speerit. Even Ike Yancy don't walk rough around her. 'God blast 'er,' says Ike.

'She's my kin, but she's a handful. I don't want none of her,' Ike says."

"Your name Blackie?"

"Anything wrong with it? What's your'n?"

"Tabor," Brad said, and he quirted the horse on as the mule-skinner gaped in astonishment.

IV

In Jericho Cañon a creek raced toward the valley. Prospect holes scarred the steep side slopes. When Brad reached the Tabor mine, he knew it at a glance. Sweat-streaked horses and armed riders and men on foot milled in front of a small log building that seemed to be the mine office.

Brad judged the property with a sweeping look. The tunnel mouth disgorged narrow rails for ore cars. A mill pile of second-grade ore towered off to the left. There were log cabins and tents for the miners. There was a small donkey engine, an ore crusher, a grizzly, and a sorting table under an open-sided structure. It looked what it was, a new mine, under development.

Then Brad forgot the mine. Anger and explosive threat charged the air in front of the small log office. Miners, teamsters, and prospectors from all along the cañon seemed to have gathered here. Shaffer and his men were on their horses in a tightly watchful knot before the office. They surrounded Steve Williams.

Orrie Simms and armed deputies faced them. A third small group of armed men were to the left of them. Sally Williams was with that third group on a run-out sorrel horse. She had slipped on a riding skirt and soft doeskin jacket. She was dusty and she looked tired. But there was a suppressed blaze of purpose about her. She gave one look as Brad came up fast, then her eyes went back to the Candlestick men and her brother.

Everyone else watched Brad come up. He felt the weight of it come out and meet him. Even Orrie Simms swung his horse and waited. Men on foot got out of the way. No one had any welcome. Hair-edged tempers merely paused.

Orrie Simms's tone was sarcastic. "Thought you meant to light a shuck."

"I did," Brad said. "Back to the Eagle House where I had a room." He pulled the blowing horse up between the Candlestick men and the sheriff's men.

Shaffer's rash, abrupt question came at him. "Was the old man dead when you left town?"

"No," Brad said. "What are you doing with that Ladder P man?"

"Keep out of this," Shaffer said with repressed roughness. "I brought him along to see who shot Tabor. I'll handle it."

Brad steadied the winded horse and started a cigarette. "I heard that Kirkland shot him."

Shaffer's answer was curt with anger. "Riggs, the bookkeeper here, and some of the mine men here saw Kirkland and Tabor ride off together. Kirkland didn't have a gun. His six-gun and rifle are in there by his desk."

Brad lit the cigarette and glanced at the grimness on Orrie Simms's leathery face. "Let the law handle this, Shaffer."

"I said keep outta this, mister. Candlestick can handle any yellow-dog moves by the Kemstead bunch. I've got my orders if it happened. Had 'em for years."

"I don't doubt," Brad said. "Who gives your orders if Kingsley Tabor is dead?"

"I'll think about that when I see dirt on his coffin."

They had roped Steve Williams's hands behind him. He was a broad-shouldered young man a year or so older than Sally. He sat his horse with a kind of poker sullenness, ringed with Candlestick guns.

"Maybe Williams is guilty," Brad said. He could feel the explosive silence as men watched him and listened. He was Brad Tabor. They were wondering about him. "If he's guilty," Brad said, "let Bo Kemstead back him against the law. Which I don't think Kemstead will. He's neighborly to Candlestick and we won't mix in."

There was shock in the silence that followed. Shaffer seemed to swell. His cold reserve boiled up and exploded.

"Neighborly, hell, you yellow-bellied young fool! Old King'd bust his coffin if he knowed Candlestick had a Tabor loaded with coyote like this. You're worse than your old man. He was soft, too. Git outta here. I've had my belly full of you."

Jip Haines headed the Kemstead group. He had the long, slab-jawed, close-eyed look of his brother, Bo Haines, who had been breaking the horse at Ladder P this morning. Jip's quick grin was pure enjoyment. Other faces had the same look as they watched a Tabor told off by a Tabor man.

Brad sat a moment, making up his mind, knowing what happened next would delay trouble or start it beyond any stopping. He spoke carefully. "Shaffer, ride down toward the road with me."

"Ride, hell! I'm busy here. Git going. Don't stop this side of California."

"Afraid of me?"

Shaffer said: "Boys, hold everything. Don't git bluffed while I settle this." He wrenched his horse out past Brad's horse, crowding. He was coldly furious and contemptuous. "Come on! Let's git it over with."

Shaffer stopped near the road and waited. Brad pulled up, facing him.

"Shaffer, you're too good a man to fire. You wouldn't have been on Candlestick so long if you weren't. But you're too mouthy. Now back it up. Pull your gun."

"Listen, you young . . ."

"Shut up," Brad said. "Back up your talk."

"I ain't going to kill a Tabor."

"You tried it with your mouth. Play it out."

Shaffer went for his gun. The roaring report that followed echoed up Jericho Cañon. Shaffer looked stupidly down at his empty gun hand. Then at the ground where his six-gun had spun. Blood started to drip slowly from the hand. Shaffer looked from the blood to the worn old cedar-handled gun Brad was sliding back in the holster. Neither man said anything until Shaffer sucked a hard breath, and spoke in a flat voice. "I aimed to try that on you. Am I fired?"

"Not by me, Shaffer, even if I had the say-so. I want the law working fast."

Shaffer thought it over. "You ain't yellow," he said shortly. He shook blood from the hand, grimaced, and sucked another hard breath. "By God, I don't know what you are, but I'll take a chance the old than lives and likes it." Shaffer's shout carried up the slope. "Turn that Ladder P man over to the sheriff!"

Orrie Simms did his part as if nothing had happened. He fired rapid questions at the bookkeeper and the Tabor miners, and went into the mine office with Brad and Shaffer and Jip Haines to see Kirkland's rifle and gun belt.

"Tabor rode up like he was looking for trouble," Orrie began to list what they knew. "He sent the bookkeeper out and stayed in here with Kirkland for nigh half an hour. Then Kirkland saddled a horse and they rode up the cañon toward the Kemstead mine and nobody saw a gun on Kirkland. Guess we better ride up the cañon to where it happened."

The Kemstead men kept together on the ride. Shaffer and his men rode apart from them. Brad rode with the sheriff a little, talking, and then dropped back. It was late in the afternoon. Sunlight struck the high rocks and trees far above. In the cañon bottom the different parties advanced through puddling shadows in wary truce. It was as if explosive angers had been frozen for a little. No man had changed his opinion. They were only waiting.

Sally Williams rode beside her brother, talking. Steve's hands had been untied but the same poker sullenness was in the set of his head and shoulders. Presently Sally wheeled her horse out and fell in with Brad when he came up.

She looked pale and young in the shadows, and troubled. "I was wrong," she said a bit defiantly. "You could have killed those men who held up the stage."

Brad grinned suddenly. He needed this moment. "It didn't seem worthwhile with my arms full of pretty wildcat."

Sally flared: "Stop making fun of me. I'm worried about Steve."

"I'm worried about Ladder P breaking loose against Candlestick," Brad said, sobering again. "Where's Ike Yancy?"

"Ike was at the mine when Steve and Denver Jack started to Piedras."

"So his name is Denver Jack. He's not a polite gent. What does he do?"

"He works for Ike," Sally said absently. She was thinking. She said abruptly: "Thanks for helping Steve." She rode on ahead and fell in with her brother again and talked earnestly. Steve shook his head at her almost angrily.

Brad rolled and lit a cigarette, and turned back and fell in with Shaffer. "What do you know about this Denver Jack?"

"Hired gunman," said Shaffer briefly. He had bandaged his hand out of the mine medicine chest and his reserve was back. "The Kemsteads keep a few of them around."

"Why didn't you bring him along with Steve Williams?"

"He wasn't around when we collared young Williams. We had all we needed."

41

"The sheriff says Steve wasn't armed when he reached Piedras."

"Makes me sure he did it," said Shaffer, unrelenting. "Ain't any other reason he'd have got rid of his guns at such a time. He knew hell would pop after a Kemstead brought King Tabor into town dead or dying."

Shaffer waited a minute. His question was blunt. "You came into Piedras on the stage with that gal. Did it make you partial to the Kemsteads?"

"No," Brad denied. "Just to her."

Shaffer's cold reserve cracked for an instant in the ghost of a smile. "Twenty years ago I could talk like that. She serves good food."

"Twenty years ago you wouldn't have thought about your belly," Brad guessed.

Shaffer's chuckle sounded like it didn't come often. "I was a pistol." Then Shaffer's face hardened. "She's a Kemstead, even if she did go on her own in Piedras."

They had been riding through a short gorge with rock slides rising sheer for hundreds of feet. The men ahead were stopping in a widening curve on beyond. Steve Williams was talking to Orrie Simms and gesturing.

Brad spurred up and joined them. Orrie said to him: "Kingsley was here in the road when Steve and Denver Jack found him. Kemstead's Number One mine is less'n a mile ahead. Steve says they were this side of the mine when they heard the shots. Two shots, you say, Steve?"

Steve Williams nodded with sullen indifference.

"Kirkland was gone," Orrie went on. "Just ahead there the Blue Lake trail takes off up the side of that shoulder. It's the only way Kirkland could have gone on his horse."

"Where does the trail go?"

"Up above timber to Blue Lake," Orrie said. "It's bad country

42

to head into without grub or blankets or a gun like Kirkland seems to have done." Orrie pulled his right ear-lobe thoughtfully. "Got to have Kirkland," he decided. "Where's Bill Janes?" He looked around. "Bill! Take Steve Williams back to Piedras and lock him up. Better stop at the mine and get Kirkland's gun belt and rifle. Lock up that Denver Jack, too, if you find him. Give me your rope. I'm going after Kirkland."

Bill Janes had a broad round face with one cheek full of tobacco. He nodded. "You ain't got any grub or blankets, Orrie. Be night soon."

"Kirkland ain't got 'em, either," said Orrie. "Sit on everything until I get back."

"I'll ride along," Brad stated.

Jip Haines spoke in a low voice to several of the men with him and said loudly: "I'll go, too!"

"Just you two," Orrie Simms said. "I'll be traveling fast. Can't be bothered."

They left with no more than that. From high up on the first rocky shoulder of mountain Brad looked down at the armed riders lingering in the cañon bottom. The restrained violence still seemed to hang about them.

Orrie Simms pushed his horse to the limit up toward the high, lingering sunlight. The narrow trail skirted dangerous drops and washed spots. The cañon road was far behind and below when Orrie dismounted and studied fresh sign in the trail.

"Kirkland sure came this way," Orrie announced briefly, mounting again.

Jip Haines followed him in tight-lipped silence. Brad brought up the rear. Once Brad dismounted and studied more sign in the trail. Jip Haines watched him and rode on when Brad mounted again.

They reached silver-trunked aspens. The thinning air chilled as light faded. The horses, pushed hard, were showing it, when Orrie Simms turned off the trail. He followed a small run of seep water, and rode through brush into a steep sloping mountain meadow shadowy in the last twilight.

"Looks like his horse ahead there," Orrie said quietly.

They had the horse a few minutes later. It had been grazing with the saddle turned under its belly. Orrie got down, tested the cinches, and grumbled: "Fool mine man. Loosened his cinches, turned the saddle, and hoped we'd figure he fell off back along the trail." Orrie pulled his ear-lobe again. "No gun. He's afoot. It's getting dark."

Orrie righted the saddle, cinched it tight, and climbed back on his horse, holding the heavily knotted reins of Kirkland's grazing horse.

"Going back?" Jip Haines inquired quietly.

"Nope," said Orrie briefly. "Keep close when it's dark. I know where I'm going."

Almost two hours later Orrie dismounted among more aspens and guardedly told them to tie the horses and follow on foot. They had come a treacherous way without benefit of trail. Orrie at times had seemed in doubt himself in the dark. Now there was only enough starlight to show the pale aspen trunks and the man walking ahead.

Orrie stopped again. His voice was more guarded but satisfied. "Smoke smell. There's an old cabin ahead, backed up against a rock outcropping. Old man Butler used to hole up here while he was prospecting. Only place I know of that a man on foot could have reached tonight. I'll go ahead."

They reached grass and open space under the stars. The dark outcropping of rock was visible, then the low bulk of a small cabin as they advanced. Orrie Simms had faded out ahead. The faint smoke smell drifted to them again. Orrie's voice suddenly lifted, sharp and clear.

"This is the sheriff, Kirkland! Open up!" Then Orrie called: "I'm coming in, Kirkland!"

Brad ran. Jip Haines kept with him. They heard Orrie Simms swearing inside, and, as they reached the open door, a match flared in the cabin. Orrie exclaimed: "I run in and fell over him! Damned if he ain't blowed his head open."

Brad grabbed for matches and stepped in, lighting one. Jip Haines followed with more light. The body was there at their feet, revolver in the right hand and dark blood pooled on the beaten dirt floor.

"He didn't have a gun," Brad pointed out.

Jip Haines's short laugh was a sneer. "That ain't a whittled stick in his right hand, mister. Unless he had extra cartridges along, there oughta be three shells fired. Two for King Tabor. One for him."

Jip Haines was right. Orrie Simms had found a candle stump and lit it. When all three had examined the fired shells, Jip spat with satisfaction. "He had the gun hidden on him somewhere. He got this far and his nerve gave out. Simms, you better get to Piedras quick and turn Steve loose before Bo Kemstead builds a fire under you. There's a shorter way out that turns in near the head of Jericho Cañon." Jip spat again and eyed them through the candlelight, grinning. "I knew you were heading here. Bo grubstaked old Butler. He knew the old half-wit hung out up here three, four years ago. This oughta cure you of taking orders from Candlestick."

"It ain't cured me of anything but taking you along," Orrie Simms retorted sourly. "Help get the horses and we'll load him on."

Jip was still jeering. "Bring him in yourself. It's your job. I aim to ride straight down past the mine and into Piedras and spread the word of what a fool you were to take orders from

Shaffer and the Candlestick bunch. I'll laugh in Shaffer's face myself."

Jip swaggered out and kept going, whistling in high humor.

Brad said: "He'll start trouble. Shaffer and his men are ready for it."

"He'll try," Orrie growled. "But Bo Kemstead ain't the fool some of those smart nephews think he is. Bo bellows. He'd fight Candlestick at the wink of an eye. But I was the one who locked Steve Williams up. Bo'll wait for me."

"I hope so," Brad said.

He reached for the flickering candle stump and looked around the small room, and at the body and the bullet hole in the right temple. He walked outside and around the cabin.

Orrie Simms was standing glumly in the doorway when Brad came back and returned the candle.

"Sheriff, if it'll make you feel any better, you won't have to turn Steve Williams loose. Or Denver Jack, if he's locked up. Bo Kemstead will be lucky if he's not locked up, too."

"What's that?" Simms almost shouted.

"Tell you when we get back to Piedras."

"I've got to know now."

Brad stood soberly and shook his head. "I grew up thinking the trouble between Tabor and Kemstead was mostly foolishness. I thought a sensible head could end it." Brad rolled a quick cigarette as he talked. He lit it and threw the match down hard and said bitterly: "Now I'm the one who will probably start Bo Kemstead shooting. I've got to think about it."

Simms peered past the wavering candle flame. "Sounds like you're sure of what you're saying."

"I am," Brad said almost savagely, and went to get the horses.

V

They came down Jericho Cañon in deep night with Kirkland's body lashed across his own saddle. Men hailed them at the Kemstead mine and gathered around as they dismounted.

"Where's Ike Yancy?" Orrie Simms inquired.

"Him and Jip Haines lit out for Piedras," a man holding a lantern answered. "Yancy says there's a light mule wagon and a driver to haul the body in if you want to ride fast from here."

"I mean to," said Orrie Simms grimly. "How about fresh saddle horses?"

"All we got is the two Yancy and Haines left. They're beat out, too." The man was grinning. "You in a hurry to turn Steve Williams out?"

Brad looked around while they talked. What he could see of this Kemstead mine was about the same as the Tabor mine. Big wagons loaded with ore bulked nearby in the night. Among the men standing around was the red-faced muleskinner with the raspy voice who had come into Sally Williams's restaurant. The man looked him over and grinned and turned away.

A few minutes later on the rough cañon road again, Orrie Simms growled: "The whole damned bunch was laughing at me! I hope you knew what you were talking about up there on the mountain!"

"You'll see," Brad said.

They found lights at the Tabor mine on farther down the cañon and Brad guessed: "King Tabor's horse should be here. Probably another one. I'll stop and look at Kirkland's books."

Orrie Simms got his fresh horse and rode on fast toward Piedras. Brad went into the mine office and looked swiftly through ledgers and asked questions of the bowlegged little bookkeeper, Riggs.

"Any idea what King Tabor said to Kirkland?" Brad asked.

Riggs had a sad-looking brown mustache. He was nervous

and anxious to please, but he shook his head. "Mister Tabor sent me out while they talked." Riggs hesitated. "Will the mine stay open?"

Brad made absent marks on the edge of the bookkeeper's high desk with a piece of chalk he had picked up. He was thinking hard.

"Work the same as usual," he decided. "I see three loaded ore wagons out there. You shipping tomorrow?"

"Yes, sir. Shipping every week lately."

Brad finished a few minutes later. He walked out and looked at the ore wagons, then went to the fresh saddle horse at the office hitch rack. It was King Tabor's fine gray horse, rested and full of run. He had a hand on the saddle horn when a big, bearded figure came up. It was the muleskinner named Blackie. The big man chuckled.

"Mister, I didn't know who you was on the road today. You gonna be boss now?"

"Stop in Piedras tomorrow and ask me," Brad said, swinging up.

"By God, I will, mister. I like to know where my bread is buttered."

Brad rode toward Piedras. Brad let the horse run. The long smooth gallop overtook the mule-drawn ore wagon carrying Kirkland's body and left it far behind.

A few faintly winking lights marked Piedras in the distance ahead when a quirted horse broke out of the vague starlight. The rider pulled up hard as they met.

"Brad? Brad Tabor?"

"Good Lord. Sally!" Brad wrenched the gray horse around and joined her.

Sally urged: "Ride off the road quick. Don't ask questions. This way."

Brad followed her north of the road until Sally dismounted

and said in a tight voice: "They weren't far behind me. Listen." At first there was nothing but their own hard-blowing horses. Then Sally's hand went to his arm in tense warning. Brad heard it—the rapid beat of several horses, galloping toward Jericho Cañon. They passed the spot where Sally had met him and faded toward the cañon.

"I think they're trying to kill you," Sally said unsteadily. She jerked her hand from his arm when Brad reached for it. "I should have let them. You're better dead than alive, Brad Tabor."

Brad wheeled and held her shoulders. "Sally, tell me about it."

She had on the same soft doeskin jacket and no hat. The night hid the copper softness of her hair, and when his hands tightened, Sally stiffened. Then she came against him, her cheek against his chest, her hands on his arms high up. They were trembling. Her unsteady voice had a note of despair as she talked.

Brad touched her hair a time or two and asked sober questions, until he had all the news of Piedras. Sally suddenly pushed away. Her resentment flared at him. "You're trying to have Steve hanged for something he didn't do!"

"Sounds like Jip Haines and Ike Yancy really stirred up the Kemsteads and the whole town, too, including you," Brad said evenly. "You say King Tabor still can't talk and may die any minute, and Orrie Simms has locked the jail till morning, with Steve still in it, on my say-so. Listen, Sally . . . jail is the best place for Steve right now. Bo Kemstead and his nephews are in worse trouble than they think. Ike Yancy knows it. Why else would he take men and ride to kill me?"

Sally said huskily: "They want Steve out."

"I never saw Ike Yancy," Brad reminded. "Why should Yancy want to kill me just because the sheriff took my word for something?" She made no answer and Brad continued: "Yancy wants me killed because he's afraid of what I might know. Who does that make guilty? I'm not trying to kill anyone."

The despair came back in Sally's voice. "I don't know what to believe. But I knew all along Steve shouldn't stay on the ranch with them."

"Why not?" Brad asked quickly.

"They moved in on Uncle Bo like buzzards," Sally said with pent-up bitterness. "They're greedy and selfish and they hate one another because they don't know who's going to get the most when Uncle Bo dies. I think he lets them stay because he's getting old and lonesome. But he tells them what they should think."

"That why you moved to town, Sally?"

"Yes. As soon as I saw how it was at the ranch, I moved to Piedras. Steve wouldn't come because he likes ranching. Now he's in trouble."

"Bad trouble," Brad agreed. "It's worse because it's mixed up with Bo Kemstead and King Tabor hating each other so long." He thought a moment, watching her. "Sally, if Steve is innocent, maybe I can pull him out of it in the morning. That is, if the Kemsteads don't get me first."

"Why can't you do it tonight?" Sally challenged.

"Orrie Simms has locked up for the night, you said. Anyway, I want to wait until morning. I've got a reason. Call me contrary."

"You're a Tabor and want your way," Sally said angrily.

Brad chuckled. "I'm a Tabor from California, where the girls aren't half so pretty and never ride out to stop a killing. You saved a Tabor tonight . . . and he's this grateful."

Brad reached quickly and drew her close. For a moment Sally clung, and then she pushed away, rubbing his kiss from her mouth. Her voice shook. "Don't do that again, Brad Tabor."

"Maybe I won't have the chance," Brad said.

She knew what he meant. She stood in the starlight, looking at him, and then almost ran to her horse and mounted and slashed with the rein ends. The fast gallop faded toward town before Brad went to his horse.

He headed on away from the Jericho Cañon road. The Kemstead men would meet the wagon with Kirkland's body and hear they had missed him. They would turn back, hunting him.

Hours later the sun was climbing high when Brad headed for Piedras again, across the range from the northeast. He had slept on the ground as he was, in a narrow winding draw in the foothills. When the sun had touched his face, he had ridden to the highest ground around, and had sat smoking, thinking, and looking into the blue distance from Jericho Cañon in the east to the great sweep of range beyond Piedras, toward Candlestick and Ladder P. Kingsley Tabor had looked out like this a lifetime ago, and had stayed and held his share of the range with bitter strength. This morning he might be dead. But for Sally Williams, Brad Tabor would be dead, too.

Far dust marked riders and an occasional wagon headed toward Piedras. Brad's smile was a hard understanding slit for a moment. They were gathering to see the showdown between Candlestick and Ladder P.

Heavier dust lifted where ore wagons moved down from the mines. Brad looked that way while he smoked a last cigarette, and then he rode off the high ground toward Piedras.

Violence was like a gun cartridge; it could look quietly harmless until the explosion. The town had that look when Brad rode in from the north. Hitch racks were full. Saloons were busy. Men stood in the open, talking. A stranger would have seen only peace.

Brad caught the repressed violence as he passed at an easy

trot. It was in the hasty turn of men who watched him silently. In the quick break other men made into saloons with word of his arrival.

Shaffer was standing in front of the doctor's office. "How is he?" Brad asked from the saddle.

"The same," Shaffer said evenly. "What do we do?"

"Steve Williams still in jail?"

"Yep. Ladder P men all in town. Bo Kemstead is getting meaner."

"Keep your men out of it, Shaffer. They'll only make it a whole lot worse."

"Can't be worse."

"Keep them out anyway."

Shaffer's silence had cold rebellion as Brad turned the gray horse back along the street. He sat in the saddle for a moment before Sally's Grub Box, scanning the street.

The heavy ore wagons had not rolled into town. More men were out in the open now. Standing. Waiting. Watching him dismount. Sally Williams looked out the window as he ducked under the rack bar. Brad went in smiling. "Eggs, please, ma'am . . . and some coffee."

Two men got up from the counter, paid, and walked out. Others had evidently just left. Dishes with food on them were still on the counter.

"I saw you ride by," Sally said, and suddenly she hit the counter with her small fist. "You fool, Brad Tabor! Get with the sheriff and stay with him. Ike Yancy and the others have been looking for you since last night."

"That's why I didn't come into town. Wasn't ready."

"Why do you think those men went out when you came in? They knew it was dangerous to be close to you."

Brad grinned. "Mighty dangerous last night, wasn't it?"

Sally flushed, and then turned her head, listening intently.

Her color drained away. Brad heard it, too—the sound of many hoofs pounding hard along the street. He slid off the stool.

"I wanted one more look at you, Sally. Remembering wasn't enough."

She was standing in numb silence as he walked out. He didn't know it but his back was pine-straight, his face had settled hard, matching coldness in his eyes. He walked out as King Tabor might have walked when a young man.

Sally Williams closed her eyes for a moment. Then she began to take off her apron with shaking hands.

They were coming in a whirl of dust and horses from the direction of the courthouse. Brad had barely time to rein the gray horse out from the hitch rack. He saw the long old figure of Orrie Simms in the van and waited watchfully.

Bo Kemstead sided the sheriff, worn black hat turned up in front, dressed like a line-camp rider on wages. But even at a distance the man had a massive force that went with command. He was backed by Ladder P men and nephews.

Orrie Simms reached the spot first and pulled up hard. His anger lashed out. "Where the hell you been?"

Bo Kemstead's roughness piled through that. "Don't matter where he's been. We got him now, damn his lying Tabor face."

The big man rode in close, shoving out his jaw. He was Bo Kemstead who had shot his starving cattle in the long blizzard rather than take favor from a Tabor. His bellow filled the street with curious men.

"Asking me if I'm a thief and a liar. Then lying my nephew Steve into jail yourself. I'll learn you what happens when a Tabor tricks Bo Kemstead."

Orrie Simms tried to take command. "Now wait a minute, Bo."

"Wait, hell. Steve's waited all night." The bellow came at Brad again. "Speak out, damn you! Don't sit looking like old

Tabor did the first day I seen him. I showed him the tally then. I'll give you worse, you low-down, lying pup."

"Where's Ike Yancy?" Brad asked coldly.

He knew the man even as he asked it. Ike Yancy was the biggest, the oldest, the best dressed of the men who backed Bo Kemstead. Yancy wore black broadcloth. His black flat-crowned hat had a rattlesnake skin around the base of the crown. A broken nose was hardly noticeable in the flat, grinning ferocity of heavy features. Yancy was grinning. His black coat was open over the gun belt beneath as he forced his horse up beside Bo Kemstead. "I'm Yancy."

"Howdy," Brad said coldly. "I hear you make mining pay for Bo Kemstead."

"Might be so."

"Are you the one who told Steve and Denver Jack to bring Tabor into the doctor?"

"That's right."

"Where were you about dark yesterday?"

"I rode over to the claims in Black Gut Cañon."

"Who'd you see over there?"

"None of your business," Yancy said,

Bo Kemstead bellowed again: "This ain't got anything to do with Steve! Speak out!"

Orrie Simms was listening, his temper checked into impassiveness. Up the street, the first ore wagon was swinging ponderously toward them on the long haul to Three Wells and the railroad.

Brad spoke to Bo Kemstead: "You fired Kirkland."

"Ike done that. He didn't need Kirkland."

"You hired Denver Jack for a gun guard."

"Ike done that, damn it. Ike runs the mines. I'm a cowman. What's all this got to do with Steve in jail?"

Straining mule teams were swinging a second ore wagon

toward them. The muleskinner was big Blackie. His snaking bullwhip drove gun-like reports along the street.

Brad lifted his voice past Bo Kemstead. "Bo Haines! Did Denver Jack return those Army gloves he borrowed from you?"

"Hell, no. I give 'em to . . ." Bo Haines broke off angrily. "That's a damn' fool question!"

"Sheriff," Brad said, "when the stage was held up, who did I tell you to look for?"

"A man who wore old Army gloves and might've been shy a little finger on the left hand. His glove finger stuck out like there was nothing inside it when he closed his left hand."

"Denver Jack," said Brad coldly, "has got all his fingers. Yesterday when he walked into Sally's place carrying a rifle in the left hand, the little finger stuck out like it was stiff and wouldn't bend in."

Ike Yancy had stopped grinning. Brad looked past him. The third ore wagon was swinging into the street. The first and second wagons had stopped. The muleskinners were talking to townsmen and staring at the bunched riders.

Men were massed along both sides of the street, keeping back near doors where they could duck for cover.

Bo Kemstead seemed to freeze in the saddle as Brad's words hung between them. His chin thrust out belligerently.

Orrie Simms was still impassive. "I looked for a nubbin finger. Never thought of a stiff one."

Brad said: "When the strangers started coming in, King Tabor had cattle rustled. He lost many shipments. He lost money mining. He borrowed and sold cattle and still he was going broke."

"Got what he deserved," Bo Kemstead growled.

"Kemstead," Brad said, "I rode over and took you like I found you. Not a thief. Not a liar. Just a stubborn old Texan mossback who didn't like King Tabor."

"Like ain't the word."

"You know what happened up Jericho Cañon," Brad said. "Sheriff, I want you and Kemstead to hear me ask those mule-skinners something."

Ike Yancy said loudly: "This ain't getting Steve free."

"Shut up, Ike," Bo Kemstead ordered. "Let him play his hand out."

All the riders followed. The muleskinners watched them come. Big Blackie coiled his long whip and called: "You settled who's boss yet, young feller?"

"I'm settling it," Brad said, pulling up by the wagon. "What time did you leave the Tabor mine?"

"Afore sunup."

"See the Kemstead wagons on the road?"

"They're coming in behind us."

Brad turned his head. "Sheriff, what did Jip Haines say when we found Kirkland dead and I said Kirkland didn't have a gun?"

Orrie Simms tugged at his ear, thinking. "Jip said that wasn't no whittled stick in Kirkland's right hand."

"You've got Kirkland's gun belt? The one we looked at in the office?"

"Yep."

"Kirkland left his horse up on the mountain and headed on foot to an old empty cabin," Brad said. "Nothing there, unless he expected a horse and grub and help to get away. His holster back at the mine was worn left-handed. The bookkeeper says he was left-handed in everything. . . ."

"By Godfrey!" Orrie Simms exclaimed. "A right-hand shot killed him. And Steve Williams was locked in jail at the time."

"If someone killed Kirkland and put the gun in his right hand, then Kirkland didn't have a gun when King Tabor was shot," Brad said coldly. "But Kirkland had to know who shot Tabor. It had to be a man Kirkland couldn't report to the law. All Kirkland could do was light up the trail fast without grub or a gun and wait at the cabin for help. And if the law thought Kirkland killed himself at the cabin, then there wasn't anyone to talk. Kirkland got all the blame."

"By Godfrey," Orrie Simms said again.

"Someone rode down that Blue Lake trail just before Kirkland rode up it," Brad said. "The sign is there in a few spots if you look close. Someone rode down that trail and met Kirkland and King Tabor and heard trouble was coming, and shot Tabor and told Kirkland to get up to cabin and wait. Steve Williams evidently came along and never did get the straight of it, and if he did start guessing, he kept his mouth shut."

"That all you got to say," Bo Kemstead asked harshly.

"Not all," Brad said firmly. "At the California mines I heard about a trick that worked for a while on high-grade ore. Two mine bosses were in on it. Muleskinners had to get their cut. One mine shipped out high-grade and the other mine low-grade ore, on the same day over the same road the 'skinners swapped wagons along the road. One mine got credit for all the high-grade that went out from both mines. The other mine lost money, like Kirkland's mine has been losing. Last night I chalked crosses under the wagon beds of the three Tabor ore wagons."

The silence, suddenly, was explosive. Bo Kemstead held reins in left hand. That left hand gripped the saddle horn until knuckles were bone white. The big man was bent forward a little in silent rage, worse because it was silent in that massive bellowing man.

Brad ran a look over the others. They were watching Bo Kemstead in tense fascination, waiting.

Brad swung down off the gray horse. He felt tight inside, cold and hard. This was the moment. This was fifty years of the past come to a head. "Kemstead," Brad said coldly, "step down with the sheriff and look. Maybe we'll see why King Tabor and Kirkland had to be shot so Ladder P could come out top dog for you and your nephews."

Orrie Simms drawled: "Bo, you've bellered. Now climb down. Let's look."

Ike Yancy heeled his horse to one side. Bo Kemstead stared down at Brad. His voice had the slow rasp of a file on metal. "Like old King himself that first day. Calling me a thief and a liar. Making it stick by showing me his home brands on strays I'd swept up and meant to keep. Looking at me like I was a mangy wolf he wouldn't touch . . . until I showed him he'd met a real wolf."

"Climb down, Bo," Simms ordered.

Bo Kemstead sat his horse, not moving. His slow rasping voice began to rumble. "That's the last time any man ever called me thief or liar. Now a Tabor's done it again. And worse. Made it stick."

Bo Kemstead's loud voice was ringing along the street. It exploded suddenly. "Damn you to the pits of hell, you black-hearted lying snake!"

Kemstead savaged the reins and drove his spurs hard. He came up in the stirrups and his right hand swung the heavy braided quirt that could cut furrows in tough horsehide. Brad and Orrie Simms dodged from the flying hoofs of the spinning horse. Through the noise Brad could still hear the screaming whistle of the braided quirt lash and its meaty cut to the bone across Ike Yancy's flat face.

Blood sprang crimson from a great slantwise furrow across Yancy's face, from hair to chin, blood in the right eye and across the nose and spurting from a sliced corner of his mouth. Yancy roared with the pain and reeled over in the saddle. His horse reared with the hard-sawed bit. His outflung arm was too late to stop the second whistling slash of the terrible quirt. And there was a second furrow to the bone that would mark the flat face to the grave. Yancy screamed this time. He clawed under his coat for the holstered gun.

Bo Kemstead's bellowing fury missed the move or ignored it. Brad snatched his own gun. He had to step fast to one side as Kemstead's horse plunged in front of the target. At that it was a trick shot. Only half of Yancy was visible, with Bo Kemstead in between. The bullet smashed Ike Yancy's shoulder. Yancy's own roaring gun fired wide into Bo Kemstead's horse. The horse went down among the other horses, throwing Kemstead hard.

In that shouting, trampling tangle of riders and horses and guns being drawn, Brad sighted Jip Haines trying to rein his horse steady. The man's cocked six-gun was lined down at Kemstead. A man had to see it to believe it. Brad might have been the only one who did see. Sally Williams's bitter, pent-up knowledge flashed to mind. *They moved in like buzzards . . . greedy, selfish . . . waiting for Bo to die. . . .* They'd own Ladder P with Bo Kemstead dead. Ike Yancy had almost made sure of Candlestick, too. Brad swung his gun fast toward the slab-faced Haines. Something that bit like fire whistled and coiled around his gun hand. The shock of it ran up his arm. The gun was torn out of his grip. Then he saw the bullwhip lash that had snaked out and snatched his gun. Brad whirled, knowing who he would see.

Haines's gun crashed out behind him. And a step to the right Orrie Simms was coming around fast, too. They both saw big Blackie, the muleskinner, drop the bullwhip and plunge toward shelter behind the heavy ore wagon.

Orrie Simms shot twice from his belt line. Through the back wheel spokes Brad saw the black-bearded figure dive into the road dust and roll limply, thrashing a little.

Orrie Simms had to shout through the tumult: "Git your gun! You're a deputy!"

Then Orrie seemed to shudder through all his long, lean

frame. A queer twisted look ran over his face as the more distant
bark of a rifle shot reached them.

"By Godfrey!" Orrie gasped. "By . . ."

Brad's eye ran the rifle down. It was held by the gun guard,
Denver Jack, who had killed the stage driver. The man was out
in the street a hundred yards away, sighting for another shot as
Orrie collapsed.

The law was down; there was no law in Piedras now. Brad
dived for the gun Orrie had dropped. His own old wooden-
handled gun had been flipped yards away by the bullwhip. There
was only Candlestick and Ladder P in roaring bloody showdown
along the dust-churned street. He came up with Orrie's gun,
with nerves and flesh set against the smashing rifle bullet that
was lined on him. A man couldn't miss with a rifle at that
distance. Denver Jack hadn't missed the stage driver the other
day, or Orrie Simms just now. He wouldn't miss Brad Tabor.

There was no rifle bullet. Brad's heart leaped hard, tight in
the throat, as he saw the slim skirted figure with copper hair.
She had come with that never forgotten boy-like litheness out of
the crowding confusion of spectators along the building fronts.
Fast and lightly into the street dust and open sunlight behind
Denver Jack, a shotgun in her hands, all the reckless lovely
wildcat in her threatening the man. *Clawing with a shotgun!*
Brad thought.

A man could think things like that while death roared and
churned around him, while bullet-smashed flesh gouted red
blood into the trampled street dust. While breath stopped, heart
died, voice went away, and knees were water from fear for her.
Denver Jack half turned toward her, his long bony face rigid,
long upper lip drawn back until sun struck the white dog teeth.
He stood there a breath as if balancing the risk—and then two
men, shamed by a girl, broke out in the open toward him, guns
drawn.

A watch's second hand could not have ticked twice around since the first screaming quirt slash. Men had died and were dying. The trampling, shouting, gun-crashing confusion spurred apart along the street, as if men were trying to find out who was killing who. There were Ladder P men hired by Bo Kemstead. Gun-hung men hired by Ike Yancy. There was a deputy or two—and there were the nephews.

Orrie Simms was down. Bo Kemstead was down, his big hand still gripping the braided quirt. Hoof-churned dust drifted like a pall. A man pitched from his horse. He looked like one of Orrie Simms's deputies. The man who shot him across half the width of the street looked like one of Yancy's gun guards.

As Brad saw that, the hammer blow of a bullet against his side knocked him staggering. He looked, and Jip Haines was there in the swirling dust, slab face grinning while he fired again. He missed as Brad staggered down on a knee.

Another rider yanked his horse around in the middle of the street. It was Ike Yancy, the deep quirt gashes cutting his blood-sheeted face into grotesque segments. Yancy's gun arm hung limply from the smashed shoulder. He handled the reins with the other hand.

A man could see them while he was giddy and numb and a leg felt helpless. A man could think while he tried to line a suddenly heavy and clumsy six-gun on his target. *The last Tabor,* Brad thought. *And then they'll have Candlestick, too.* He fired at Jip Haines. He fired twice before he saw a dark hole smash through Jip's grinning cheek bone and the back of Jip's head tear out in bone and blood and flying brain and hair. The last Tabor.

Ike Yancy's savage-spurred horse was rushing through the dust pall, huge and high, red nostrils flaring. Ike Yancy's bloody face was there still higher. Yancy's teeth were showing, nearer, higher—almost overhead as Brad got the heavy gun up and fired at the white teeth. He missed.

It was Ike Yancy's broken nose that split open, deep and all the way up between the popping eyes and through the bursting forehead. Brad tried to fall aside and was too slow. The racing horse knocked him flat, trampled him, and the sun went out and the dust pall went black. . . .

A man could think in death, even after that last blur of driving hoofs. Brad's eyes opened and everything was still black. Then he heard angry voices.

"Damn it! Ladder P gits Candlestick!"

"You're a lying low-down thief! Candlestick gets Ladder P!"

Bo Kemstead and King Tabor! Bo had died in that bloody shambles. King Tabor must have died, too. Yet they were still at it. Brad thought he heard a quick breath close by, and he lay still, listening to Bo Kemstead's angry voice.

"Months ago I had my damn' will fixed so the only honest kin I had who really liked me would get it all. She's Ladder P now, same as I am. Which means Ladder P gets Candlestick."

"He's Candlestick," King Tabor said coldly. "A man gets what he marries. So Candlestick gets Ladder P. Nobody would have got anything if Shaffer and his men hadn't come up and settled that bunch."

"Shaffer?" Brad said.

He heard a soft gasp nearby. "Brad. Are you conscious?"

"Sally? I can't see. Is it night?"

"It's morning, next day. Your eyes are bandaged."

"Where am I?"

"Doc Jones's office."

"I heard Bo Kemstead and my grandfather. Can't hear them now."

Sally sounded nervous. "They're in beds in the back room, still quarreling." Sally's voice lifted, defiantly. "I think they're enjoying it, too."

Brad groped and found a small soft hand and held it tightly. "Sally." He had to swallow hard. "Will Ladder P have Candlestick?"

She had the same heady touch of cologne water. Her hair was wondrously soft as his hand found it, while her lips came to his lips for a breathless moment. Then her warm soft cheek rested against his.

"Sally," Brad said huskily. "Sally Wildcat."

Bo Kemstead's vastly satisfied voice lifted in the back room. "You see! Ladder P gits Candlestick! Now shut up!"

★ ★ ★ ★ ★

Brand of the
Hangtown Kid

★ ★ ★ ★ ★

When T.T. Flynn recorded in the notebook he kept on his fiction that he finished this story on September 1, 1944, he knew that his agent would be sending it to Mike Tilden, editor of Popular Publications' Western pulp magazines. He knew Tilden changed the titles of stories if he scheduled them for publication, and so Flynn simply titled this one "Western" in his notation. Mike Tilden bought it on October 1, 1944 and the author was paid $180. Upon publication in *Fifteen Western Tales* (9/45) it was titled as it is above, and so the title remains for its first appearance in book form.

I

Mart Gaines had been pushing the chestnut horse across the back range with quirt and spur. Usually he was considerate of a horse and this mad ride through the dying day toward the sunset would have made his friends wonder. But presently he sighted four low-circling buzzards off to the right and swung the foam-flecked chestnut that way.

When he rode with a rush over the low rise, two more buzzards flapped clumsily from the ground and beat off in a wide circle, leaving with apparent reluctance the sprawled body of a man. Mart reined to a quick stop and struck the ground, running in his scuffed and worn half boots.

The man, a stranger, was dead—just dead and still warm. Mart dropped the limp wrist he had picked up. He was disappointed. He stood a moment, staring at the body, while the chestnut horse caught breath through flaring nostrils. The dead man was aged somewhere around forty. He was hatless; his sandy hair grew thinly. A sandy stubble of several days' growth covered the lax lines of a broad and meaty face. A faded, ripped brush jacket marked him from the thorn thicket country to the south. He wore two gun holsters, but one holster was empty. Mart stooped and broke the remaining gun. The cartridges had been fired. The man had been shot through the chest.

Mart dropped the gun, gave a last look at the body, shook his head, and swung quickly back into saddle and slashed with the braided quirt.

In the west, sunset was a riot of scarlet color. High clouds were bathed in gold and red. The sun's glare was in Mart's gray-green eyes. He squinted against its blaze, his look one of set intensity as it ranged ahead toward the somber upthrust of the Ten Dog buttes.

A little later his ranging gaze sighted a rider far ahead. He eased off the gallop until the blowing horse was trotting, and then walking. The punished horse blew less hard after a bit, and Mart put him into a trail trot, frowning. He looked down at the foam-flecked beast; the signs of the wild ride could not be hidden, and they might have to be explained. It might be asked why Mart Gaines was out here on the almost forgotten Hangtown way to the Ten Dog badlands.

Mart had hoped with some reason that he might pass this way through the last daylight without being seen. The set look in his eyes began to smolder watchfully as he neared the approaching rider. As a matter of caution, without conscious thought, Mart made certain his .45 handgun was ready for any need. He reached down and checked the smooth slip of the repeating rifle in the old leather saddle scabbard.

Finally his wide mouth twisted in a wry smile. That checked shirt and lop-brimmed black hat could only belong to Duz Wilkerson. Duz was riding easily. His right arm was in a bandanna sling. As they approached each other, Mart saw that the bandanna and the checked sleeve over the arm, and the sleeve cloth well up to the shoulder muscles, were dark with freshly dried blood, and that the long thin face of Duz Wilkerson had a stretched-out, pallid look.

Duz appeared exhausted. But the slant of cheek bones and the sharpness of Duz's nose still gave the sly, probing look that so well matched Duz Wilkerson's inquiring habits. All the Rainbow range was Duz Wilkerson's private patch of news. Duz was always rooting around to find something no one else knew.

Mart was the younger man of the two. His scuffed half boots, washed, faded overall pants, were not impressive. But Duz Wilkerson's greeting held respect and covert curiosity when they came together.

"Howdy, Duz."

"Howdy, Gaines," Duz said. "Kinda off your way, ain't you?"

"Kind of," Mart agreed. His faint smile hid nothing and invited nothing. "What happened, Duz?"

"We had a fight."

"Who had a fight?"

"Ain't you heard about the posse?"

"What posse?"

Duz was weak from loss of blood and saddle effort. But the questions fed him new strength. He visibly swelled with the importance of what he knew and Mart Gaines did not know.

"Pete Diggers has got a posse out," Duz said, resting a hand on the saddle horn and leaning forward with the importance of what he had to say. "We had a fight." Duz jerked his head back the way he had come. "A running fight that's still going on for all I know."

Mart pursed his lips in a faint whistle.

"Yes, sir," Duz said. "Pete's got nigh twenty men outta Rainbow. Pete swore every man in as deputy. He means to clean up that gun bunch alive or dead before the boys stop riding."

"What gun bunch?" Mart asked. He shifted over in the saddle and started to roll a cigarette. He nodded at Duz Wilkerson's wounded arm. "I can see there was plenty of fighting." Mart grinned without malice. "I don't suppose you shot yourself by accident."

Duz sighed. He looked annoyed. "You're darn' right I didn't shoot myself. I thought everybody around Rainbow knew what was going on."

"I'm not around Rainbow much," Mart reminded. "Foreman

69

for Cap Hollister's spread keeps me busy."

"Well, news spreads fast," said Duz. He moved the bad arm and shoulder and winced, and still did not talk about the wound. Duz always let his news out little by little, this way. He liked to hold it back, savor it, enjoy it, like a tasty bite. The glow of having something to tell was even in his pallor.

"The Myrtle City stage got robbed this morning," Duz said. "Six men done it. They meant business. Got a box of gold going to the Myrtle City bank and cleaned out the passengers. Even collected rings and watches."

"You took long enough to tell it," Mart said. He lit the cigarette. "So Pete Diggers found the gunmen. They sure made a hard ride to get over this way from the Myrtle City road and run into Pete and his men."

"Uhn-huh," Duz agreed. "But they done it. Looks like they'd have knowed word might get back to the railroad at Carson's Crossing, and go around by telegraph to South Fork, and get carried on up to Rainbow."

"So that's how Pete heard so quick."

"Yep. And Pete Diggers had him a brain wave that the gunmen might be heading this way. Pete said the best place them fellers had to ride for was the Ten Dog breaks or up around old Hangtown."

"What made Pete think that?" Mart inquired.

Duz shrugged before he thought, caught his breath at a jump of pain, and shook his head gingerly. "Darned if I know how Pete figured it. But he throwed a posse together quick. Got everybody around town who was willing to go, and fanned out to cut any fresh trail headed toward the Ten Dogs. Done it, too," Duz said with satisfaction. "The bunch I was in found tracks near Big Deep draw. They was headed west, like Pete guessed."

"Where'd you find the men, Duz?"

"Caught 'em swapping horses in the Double Loop pasture, t'other side of Horn Ridge." Duz took a breath. Color crept into his pale face from a new pride and importance. "Wasn't but seven of us run up on 'em. You never seen such a gunfight bust out in your life. We rode hell-an'-gone at 'em. Kilt one, too. I got shot up plenty."

"That arm doesn't look too good," Mart agreed. "How bad is it?"

"Plenty bad. I bled all over the place," Duz said with morbid enjoyment of the details. A thing like this had never happened to Duz before. He looked down at the arm and winced as he gingerly moved it. "I'd have stayed with the boys but I had to get home while I could ride." Duz finally came out with the thing that was prodding his curiosity. "How come you're heading out this way?"

"Taking a short cut," Mart answered, and did not say where. "Anyone in the posse know the gunman who was killed?"

"Nope. He was young feller." Duz covertly studied Mart's horse. "Looks like you been riding fast."

"This one likes to run." Mart looked toward the red sunset and the dark and gloomy masses of the Ten Dog buttes. "I ought to ride after that posse, I guess. Where was the fight heading when you left?"

"That-away," said Duz, taking in the western horizon with a jerk of his head. "They was scattered when I left. The trail's kind of hard to find. But Pete Diggers has got enough men to bring it to a showdown, maybe by dark."

"Sounds like I'll have a time finding them."

"You might." Duz took a breath. He had something else to say. He had to let it out. "No telling where lead might be coming from if you join up with Pete Diggers's posse," Duz said vaguely. "After dark it'd be hard to tell who shot who."

Duz waited, his look blank but missing nothing.

Mart laughed softly. Strength was in his jaw line. The lean length of his face suggested a restrained recklessness. His eyes were the kind that saw much and told little. Now the humor was reflected in his eyes as he lifted the reins to ride on. He gave Duz Wilkerson the answer Duz was waiting for, and would certainly repeat along the main street in Rainbow to all listeners. "I doubt if Pete Diggers would try that around his posse, or if we were alone," Mart said. And as he shook the reins, he added: "There's a dead man back there where the buzzards are circling. Bet he's one of the gunmen who was shot bad and rode off without being trailed."

"Whyn't you say so quicker?" Duz said in exasperation.

Mart lifted a hand in parting salute and put the chestnut horse into an easy run. Presently, with Duz Wilkerson about out of eye range, Mart hit with the quirt and began to ride hard again.

He did not head for the country beyond Horn Ridge where the gunmen had been caught changing horses. He swung into a dry arroyo that bore off to the right, toward the masses of the Ten Dog buttes and the shoulder of Smoke Mountain and the Indian Head range that backed Smoke Mountain. This was the old Hangtown way, which men seldom rode any more. Mart had been eight years old when he last passed this way, and yet it seemed he was on an old and familiar journey.

It was a ride back through life, through the years, through memories that hurt now because of the greater pain they had once left. Mart Gaines rode back into boyhood as the sun dropped with its gay light, below the westward horizon. Night came at him with its chill. Some of the cold was from inside, where, in his maverick days, he had known fright, terror, hurt, shame. It was all there, and more.

Mart did not try to sort out all he felt. He had started riding on an impulse, and if he had stopped to think and question himself, he might have turned back. He rode on into the higher country.

Rainbow range came up against the south-reaching masses of the Indian Head range, rolling waves of bunch grass and scrub brush against unfriendly cliffs. The Indian Heads were unfriendly. They had been so when Apaches swept down out of them in fast forays of murder and loot. They were so now. Men had gone into the Indian Heads and vanished. Outlaws who made the Indian Heads usually got away. Strayed cattle had a way of disappearing when their sign pointed into the mountains.

Hangtown had once been a prosperous mining spot, prosperous for a month. It had been called Gloriosa. Men who had come later to live in the abandoned buildings had brought the name Hangtown.

To the south the Indian Heads fell off in the sullen Ten Dog buttes, that were black basaltic rock, gloomy, threatening on the brightest day. The Ten Dog badlands, west of the buttes, were a gutted, gullied place of little grass, raw rock, eroded clay and gravel, and old lava flows. Salt flats glared with dazzling whiteness in the hot sun. Water was found only at one or two spots—and rarely.

Above it all, Hangtown perched on a high bench, which was the lip of a deep and narrow cañon. From Hangtown one could see out over Rainbow range and the Ten Dog desolation. In Hangtown one was close against the savage heights of the Indian Heads. The fight that had finally cleaned out Hangtown had been made by men gathered from all the Rainbow range. Honest men off honest cattle land. They had left Hangtown only a name and a black memory.

The stars were out as the jaded chestnut horse worked upward at a walk. He'd not gallop any more tonight. When Mart reined up in the gullied trail they were following, the horse stood with drooping head. But in a moment its ears pricked.

Mart heard it. Then, too—the flat, hard sounds of gunfire ahead, higher, where the Hangtown bench looked over Rainbow range. In the starlight his face tightened. A dull hard knot of tension formed under his belt. It was a feeling that had not been there in years, a hard tiredness, most of it inward, where emotion had been bottled and surging all the long afternoon.

He shook the reins and sent the horse on, and his head was canted intently listening to all sound ahead, putting the animal to the left of the trail, through close brush. He rode carefully, quietly. The night was thick here in the brush. It was hard to see, but the changing years had not blinded his memory. When he stopped, the shoulder of the mountain was steeper before him. The ghostly pale trunks of slender aspens rose about him. He tied the horse here and went on afoot, moving now without sound. He had the rifle, but he carried it easily, not hunting for a target.

The gunfire was sporadic. An odd shot or two would speak out, then many guns would hammer response. Ragged echoes would float back and whisper off into the far night. Quiet would follow. In that silence, drawn tight as rope between saddle horn and sprawling bull, was waiting threat. Then the guns would talk again.

New brush had grown. Trees had changed. But the mountain was the same, and his memory came stronger with each stride. He had the curious feeling that time had been wiped away. The years had not passed. He was not Mart Gaines, foreman for Cap Hollister, the toughest, hardest, wealthiest rancher in all Rainbow range. He was Marty Gaines, eight years old—and seven and six years old. The trees were towering forest giants, as they had seemed then. The mountain was a fabulous, gigantic world of threat, of joy and fear, with the sky close, and all the world far down below in mystery and danger.

II

Mart was marking the gunshots as he made his way. They were on the Hangtown bench, where the abandoned cabins had once stood around the deserted stores and saloons. They were around the workings of the old Gloriosa Mine, which drove into the mountain at the north side of the bench. The buildings had been burned after that great fight that had cleaned out Hangtown. If men were holed up there now, they were in the mine tunnel.

Pete Diggers, sheriff of Rainbow, had known what he was doing. Pete must be feeling good now—there was only one entrance to the old mine. If his posse had the tunnel mouth covered, all he had to do was wait. He'd have his prisoners, even if he didn't try to go into the mine and shoot them out.

Mart worked up over lichen-covered rocks and steep slopes until he was at the edge of the broad bench. The guns were close now, snapping viciously. There was enough starlight to make the mine entrance easily visible.

He stayed on the steep slope and worked to the left, westward. Once he was high enough to look over at the ruined cabin sites. Saplings and brush had lifted in a tangle. He sighted spurts of gunfire and several dark figures moving fast, keeping down out of sight.

He passed along a steep bank, where rusting tin cans and old beer and whiskey bottles marked the camp dump. Bottles slipped under his feet and he had to balance wildly to keep from sliding down the great slope over which he was moving. Here the Hangtown bench fell away abruptly; farther down the drop was straight for hundreds of feet. A man who went down out of control could keep going until he plunged into space.

Mart moved carefully. The tightness of danger stayed with

him after he had passed the old dump. The slope over which he was moving was steeper, if anything. It grew worse ahead.

Queer that in the long ago a boy had not been as nervous as the man was now. The boy had scrambled lightly this way, laughing at the danger below. Mart grinned faintly at the memory and kept on. He passed clear around the western edge of the Hangtown bench. The giddy upthrust of Smoke Mountain began to lift above him. The guns were behind him. He was working along a slightly sloping cliff, covered with a scanty stubble of gnarled tree growth and scrabbly bushes.

The drop below was a breath-taking threat of open space, but when Mart presently began to climb, it was as if his hands and feet were following a way they had long known. He came to a thin cleft in the mountain that sloped steeply up. He moved carefully up the cleft. It formed a chute that could launch a sliding body out into space. A hundred feet and more up the chute there was a shadowy black, door-like opening on the left. Mart stepped into it and relaxed. The damp draft that moved past him into the open had the smell of rotting wood and dark depths.

Mart chuckled softly. The gooseflesh of long ago did not come now. The man was not afraid of the dark depths of the mountain—as the boy had been.

The thick tallow candle Mart lit threw feeble light around. The rock walls and floor of the mine tunnel were damp. The candle flickered in the draft. But only yesterday men might have dumped blasted rock into the steep chute and let it roll and plunge into space below.

The cross-cut Mart turned into sloped up gradually. He made another turn, and then another, working deeper into the mine. Dull whispers ahead swelled into the harder reports of rifle shots. The sounds grew louder.

Somewhere ahead in blackness and distance a voice swore

hollowly. Mart blew out the candle and flattened against the damp rock at one side and lifted his voice.

"Big Jack! Oh, Big Jack!"

Guns went silent ahead. It was as if the mine were holding its breath. Mart thought he heard the husk of furtive voices, but was not sure. He called again.

"Big Jack! Are you there?"

"Damn it, Sam! I told you I heerd it! That's in the mine here!"

"They ain't no one in this mine! Can't be!"

"I heerd it, I tell you!"

"Big Jack!" Mart called.

"It's a haunt! There's ghosts in here!" Another voice came hollowly along the black tunnel: "Who's he callin'? What's he mean by Big Jack?"

Mart swallowed when he heard that. Belief that had kept him going ran out now. He had a spent, disillusioned feeling. All this for nothing. Then he stopped breathing. An angry rasp said: "Haunts are hell, it's the same to me. I never seen a haunt I was skeered of and never will." The harsh rasp rolled in the rock tunnel in a challenge. "Who's waitin' around here for Big Jack?"

"Marty."

"What?" the voice shouted.

"Marty."

"Marty's dead!" The voice began to swear. "It's a ghost! Can't be anything else! Been waitin' around here all these years! I seen the kid dead with my own eyes. Blood all over his face. Wouldn't never have left him if I wasn't sure he was dead. He's been waitin' here at Hangtown all these years for me to come back! I knowed there was something headin' me back!"

The first voice said wildly: "I ain't stayin' in here with no ghost. Bad enough being trapped this way, without ghosts comin' down on my back!"

"Stay where you are!" Mart called, his throat suddenly tight. "Big Jack, this is Marty and I'm not a ghost. Stay where you are. I'm going to light a candle and come on." And then Mart said: "I've still got that old wood Colt you whittled out for me."

"Holy cow. It is the kid! Got to be him! Boys, watch them guns. I'll meet the kid!"

Mart knew he was a fool to let his throat get tight this way. But when the big, stooped figure loomed up in the candlelight, guns belted, repeating rifle in one big gnarled hand, wide-brimmed hat pushed back, Mart stood speechless.

This was not the man who had been in his mind through the years. This man's mustache was white. Deep lines were etched in the long, leather-skinned, weathered face. But yet it was the man, down to the same hard, shrewd mouth.

"So you're Marty?" the big man said, peering.

And Marty answered out of the past, and habit long forgotten. "Yes, Pop . . . it's me."

"I'll be damned! You sure growed. Don't tell me you've been livin' back in the mine here, waitin' for me."

"I thought you were dead," Mart said. "Never heard anything more about you. I came in through that old rock slide that dumps out toward the badlands. Some of us kids found a way to get up in it one day."

"I forgot that slide. Didn't know a man could get in or out it." Big Jack Gaines laughed. "I changed my name and kept away from these parts. Say, kid, how'd you know I was cornered in here? Somebody recognize me?"

"I don't think so," Mart said. The tightness left his throat. His voice hardened a little. "I heard about that Myrtle City hold-up, and that the gunmen had headed this way. When I heard that the man who called orders at the hold-up had a missing little finger and gray hair, I had a hunch who he was and where he might be heading to hole up." A shade of bitterness came into Mart's words. "I knew, if you were alive, you'd still be a thief and a killer."

Big Jack Gaines laughed. "Still know your old man, don't you, Marty? But I never killed a man when his back was turned. That is, unless he was mostly out of sight in a gunfight."

"Never mind telling me what you did. You were boss of Hangtown and you haven't changed. I've always figured Mother died of heartbreak after she found out what you were. I was called the Hangtown Kid for years because of you."

"Don't get sore about it, kid. Do the other members of that posse know who I am?"

"I don't know what they know. I lit out another way from the ranch and came here alone. Figured if it were you, I'd have to see you. When I heard the guns around the mine, I was sure I was right, and they had you cornered in the mine."

"Thought we'd shook 'em off. They snuck in and had us cornered before we knowed they were around."

"How many men are in the mine?"

"Three of us. Sam Bell, a feller called Otie White, and me. The posse shot Nevada Joe before he made the mine tunnel. Couple other boys got shot when the posse come up with us." Big Jack chuckled. "Don't know whether they're dead or not. We didn't stop to tally out."

"They're dead," Mart said. "Where's the gold you got off the Myrtle City stage?"

"We hit tough luck there. It was a fake shipment. Lead bars. That Myrtle City bank is too damn' smart to get by with a trick like that." Big Jack spat. His look was narrow through the flickering candle flame. "So you got a ranch?"

"I'm foreman for Cap Hollister," Mart said shortly. "Get your men. I'll guide you out the way I came in. By daylight you should be safe."

"They got our horses, son."

"My horse is tired. I've got to ride him back to the ranch," Mart said. "I'm not supposed to be here. You know this country well enough to make out if you've got a night's start from Hangtown."

"Sounds like you don't want me around, kid."

"I don't," Mart said bluntly. "I'm working for a straight-shooter and I've never crossed the law. What you do is your own business. But I've got my life to lead."

"*Hmm,* funny you bothered to ride here."

"You're my father. I had to come as long as I thought you might be here."

The big, stooped, leather-faced man squinted in the flickering light. His hard mouth grinned at some thought. He was a stranger—and yet he was not. He was Big Jack. He was Pop. He had never been unkind. But he had been hard, strict, dangerous.

"I'll get Sam and Otie," Big Jack said, still grinning. "They don't know my name was Big Jack Gaines. I'll have to do some explaining. Wait here."

Mart was willing enough to wait. The gunfire had kept up in bursts and scattered shots that echoed hollowly through the mine as he talked with Big Jack.

Pete Diggers and the men from Rainbow were outside. Men who were friends. Men who respected Marty Gaines, as the right-hand man of Cap Hollister. Thinking about them made Mart a little sick. He belonged with them, and yet he belonged here in the mine, too. Or did he? How much of a fool was he for this night's business?

The three men came groping back toward the burning candle. Big Jack told their names. Sam Bell was short and muscular, with a black mustache. Otie White had the same kind of sly, pointed face that Duz Wilkerson had.

"It'll take a steady head to get out of here," Mart warned

them. "You can make it if you don't lose your nerve and do exactly as I do."

"Can't be any worse than being cornered in here," Otie White said with a crooked grin. "With spooks comin' at us from the dark. Let's go before they get an idea we ain't shootin' any more and rush the tunnel."

Mart tossed the candle down when they reached the opening into the old mine chute. "Take it easy," he warned. "It looks worse than it is."

He went first, edging gingerly down the chute. Big Jack followed him, a powerful man, loose-moving, steady, despite the white mustache and the rough hard years he had lived.

Warning them now and then at a tricky spot, Mart led his father along the almost sheer side of the mountain. Behind Big Jack a frightened oath rang out—a strangled cry. Small rocks slipped and rolled.

It was the short and muscular Sam Bell. Big Jack turned nimbly back and tried to catch the man. Sam Bell was too frightened to see the hand reaching in the starlight. Clawing wildly, when he should have been slow and careful, he went down in a scramble of hands and boot toes. He yelled once in terror, and the yell went out into the night against crashing gunshots on the Hangtown bench. Sam yelled once again as his body launched out into space.

Big Jack Gaines stayed braced where he was, looking down. His voice was steady as he spoke to the man behind him.

"Come past that spot careful, Otie."

"I'm skeered to move!"

"Come on. You got to try it."

Otie was stammering. "M-makes me dizzy. I'm s-skeered to try it. I'm goin' back!"

"Otie," said Big Jack calmly, "I'll kill you where you are if you start back. I don't mean to have you caught and blab what's

happened." Big Jack put his rifle on the rough rock against
which he leaned. He made sure it would not slip and drew a
revolver. "Come on, Otie. The posse won't pay attention to one
more shot. One's enough to start you after Sam."

Mart waited, jaw muscles hard. Once more out of his own
past came the memory of Big Jack's ruthless will, his hard and
cold determination to carry through any purpose. Big Jack was
still boss of Hangtown and the men around him.

Otie groaned. Then, slowly, carefully he came on. Big Jack
waited until the smaller man reached him. He holstered the
revolver, picked up his rifle, and said: "Let's go."

The posse guns had slackened off. Men were moving about
more recklessly when Mart led Big Jack and Otie past the old
camp dump and on to safer ground.

A shout floated through the night. "Come out of that tunnel!
We'll smoke you out!"

Big Jack chuckled softly. "Somebody's gonna be powerful
disappointed. Wish I could stay around and listen to what they
say when they find the coop empty."

"Better not try it," Mart warned curtly. "That sheriff is a bad
one to fool with. You ought to know that from the way he cut
your trail and outguessed you."

"He ain't the first smart sheriff I've tangled with, kid."

They moved down into the pale aspens. The chestnut horse
was waiting. Mart put his rifle in the scabbard.

"Wish I had a horse for you," he told his father. "But you'll
do all right."

"So it's good bye, kid?"

"Yes."

Big Jack's hand grip was firm. He was in good spirits. "You're
a chip off the old block, kid. Keep thinkin' about your old man."
Big Jack laughed under his breath. "Cap Hollister's Lazy W,
huh? I remember Hollister. He posted a five hundred reward

once for the men who run off some of his steers. I met him in Rainbow and tried to get him to make it a thousand so's it'd be worth a man's time to hunt. He had an idea I knowed where his steers went but he couldn't prove it. He nigh had a stroke right there in front of the Acey bar."

Mart climbed into the saddle. "Good bye," he said, and, as he reined down through the aspens, he heard Big Jack chuckling.

Cap Hollister had never mentioned a meeting with Big Jack or a reward for stolen steers. Cap's daughter had never let on she knew the name of Big Jack Gaines. But Dorothy Hollister would be that way. She'd never speak of anything that might hurt. Thinking of Dorothy made Mart think of Pete Diggers and the posse.

He had meant to ride straight for the ranch. He turned the horse up the gullied Hangtown trail and went instead to join the posse.

Flames were starting a glow in the night when he came out on the Hangtown bench. Men were dragging dead brush and throwing it on the fire in the tunnel mouth. Pete Diggers was calling orders.

Pete saw the new rider. He stared. "So you showed up?"

The firelight glinted on the balled star points of Pete's law badge. He was a young man to be sheriff. Just thirty. Lean, smooth-moving, with narrow hips, square shoulders, Pete was always clean-shaven. He was good-looking. People liked Pete Diggers. They respected Pete, as they liked and respected Mart Gaines.

Alike in many ways, Mart and Pete eyed each other in the rising firelight at the mine entrance. Between them, like threat of the flames, was an antagonism more plain than blows. Both were smiling, but men stopped to watch them. Voices quieted. The big brush fire crackled and popped in the silence.

"I heard you might need help," Mart said easily.

"You got here late."

"I met Duz Wilkerson riding back with a bad arm. He told me."

"Duz didn't know we were coming here."

"Gunfire carries a long way at night, off a mountain like this," Mart said, still smiling. "And I made a good guess where you might be."

Pete was watching him closely. Pete started to say something, and did not. He shrugged. "We've got some gunmen cornered in the mine. Killed one before they got in the tunnel. I think there's three inside. Maybe four."

"Not many," Mart commented. He looked around. "How many men with you?"

"Over twenty."

"Need me?"

"Suit yourself."

"I guess you don't," Mart decided. "I'll get back. Got to go to Rainbow tomorrow."

From the saddle Mart smiled at Pete Diggers. Greeting members of the posse who he knew, Mart rode out of the firelight to the down trail. He could feel Pete Diggers staring after him. Pete was thinking hard. It had showed on his face.

Mart had not meant to show himself to the posse. Meeting Duz Wilkerson had been luck. Now Duz could not tell anything in Rainbow that the posse men did not know. It had to be like this, and let Pete Diggers think what he would.

Mart rode down the old badly washed trail. There was no sign of Big Jack and his companion. Mart rode easily toward the home ranch, and he was not happy. He had obeyed the law of life in going to Big Jack. It had been instinctive, an urge that required no thinking. But he had broken the rules by which Mart Gaines lived, and by which men respected him. He had the feeling there would be more to this.

III

The cool dawn looked no different than any other morning. Mart slept two hours, then he was out watching the saddling. Horses were spooky, men were cursing as they wrestled with cinches and bridles. Mart looked at them with no little pride— among them Old Jim, Dood, Paso Jack, Shorty, High Tack— nine men, and the ranch was short-handed now. The best nine men on Rainbow range, or anywhere else. Most of them were older than he, but they respected Mart Gaines. They knew he could outride, outrope, outwork, outshoot any of them, and they were proud of it, like they were proud of the Lazy W.

Hollister's ranch was not the biggest in the Rainbow country. But it had good grass, it made the most money, it was the best-run ranch. All that traced back to Cap Hollister, a pint-sized measure of profane energy at sixty-two. Cap's spoken word was better than a courtroom oath. Cross-hatched wrinkles on Cap's leathery face had long ago settled in a shrewd mask with sun-squinty eyes. Cap chewed tobacco, bellowed, and moved fast. Cap was granite-hard when necessary, calm and deadly if forced to draw a gun.

Mart thought Cap Hollister was the biggest half-pint of man, with the biggest heart in all the West. It was Cap Hollister who had helped the Hangtown Kid grow into Mart Gaines of the Lazy W.

Cap came over to the saddling corral, spat, and swore in the cool dawn. "You look like the dragged-out tail of a wet fox, Mart. That chestnut horse is beat out, if I ever seen one. What kind of riding were you doing last night?"

"I rode over to Hangtown," Mart said casually. "Pete Diggers had some gunmen cornered in the old mine. Some of the men who robbed the Myrtle City stage yesterday. Duz Wilkerson told me about it."

"Hangtown?" Cap repeated. He spat again. His wrinkled face

did not change. "Get 'em?"

"I didn't stay. Pete allowed he had the men cornered and could make out with his posse."

"You made quite a ride to help Pete."

"He's the law."

"Darn' good law," Cap said, nodding. "Pete know who he had cornered?"

"He didn't say."

"*Hmm,* well I guess he got 'em. Forget this is the day Lobey Walters said he'd be in Rainbow to talk about that bunch of steers he might sell?"

"I remember."

"I want Dot to see if she can keep Lobey from skinning her on the deal. You listen in and advise her. I'll run the ranch from the front porch today. My game leg's still hurting."

Mart set his face against a smile. That old bullet wound in Cap's leg served for any excuse Cap wanted to make. Having Dot dicker alone with Lobey Walters today was Cap's way of training Dot to run the Lazy W someday. Mart could see that Dot didn't get skinned too badly, and learn a little himself. Sometimes Mart wondered if Cap Hollister knew what it meant to the former Hangtown Kid to be trusted like this with Dot and the serious affairs of the Lazy W.

He'd been an orphan after the great fight at Hangtown, with no one wanting him much. He'd knocked around Rainbow range, choring here and there for his grub. Hangtown habits had set him apart from other boys. He could swear worse than most men. He knew all about guns. He had seen men killed, listened to talk of rustling, hold-ups, gunfights, until all that seemed a natural part of life. He was ragged and some of the time dirty. When boys hooted at him, called him the Hangtown Kid, tried to bully him, he'd fought savagely, with anything at hand. He'd had his first fight with Pete Diggers when he was nine and Pete was twelve. Neither had won. Pete hadn't like him since. Shortly after that Mart had laid open the scalp of Jakie Woods. It didn't matter that Jakie was older and had started it. The axe handle Mart had used had stretched Jakie limp and bleeding. Old Man Woods had called the sheriff.

Cap Hollister had been in Rainbow when the sheriff had brought in his nine-year-old prisoner. Mart could still see Cap walking quickly into the sheriff's office, and squinting with a scowl before he spoke.

"I'm tired of hearing about this Hangtown Kid," Cap had snapped. "Boy, are you any good?"

"You're darn' tooting I'm plenty good," Mart had answered boldly, and then had clamped down on his lower lip to keep from sniveling.

"What's your name?"

"Marty Gaines."

"Had any schooling?"

"I can say the ABCs."

"Ain't enough. You go to Miss Ida Kline's house and live. Start to school. Miss Ida'll give you two bits a week and orders. You handle the two bits like a man and take the orders. When everybody else in town thinks you're as good as you think you are, come and see me. I'll have a job. You want to trade like a man that way?"

"Does she lick me?"

"Like hell, if you need it. And if you need it, you take it like a gentleman."

The sheriff had said: "Poor old Miss Ida can't handle this one. He's tough."

Cap had snorted. "He's a man and a gentleman." Cap had squinted solemnly. "I can see down inside a feller and know what's in him. Son, you willing to trade with me, man to man?"

Mart's throat could still tighten when he thought of that moment. Cap Hollister had been for him. Cap could look inside and see how he felt. They'd shaken hands on the bargain. Marty Gaines had gone to school. Miss Ida had bought him new clothes. She had been strict.

Once she had whipped him with a light buggy whip. They both cried. Mart had cried because Miss Ida dropped the whip after the second lick and ran weeping to her room. She could have cut him to bits and he'd have grinned at her until that happened.

After that Miss Ida kissed him good night each night. Miss Ida's hair had been gray. She smelled of lavender and sometimes of the lilac flowers she sewed in little packets and kept in the dresser drawers. Miss Ida sang and laughed. Her eyes had a way of shining when she looked at Mart. It made Mart feel shining inside.

When Miss Ida died, Mart was in the last grade of school and the boys hadn't called him the Hangtown Kid in years. Miss Ida had allowed him one fight a month, if someone else started it. Fists only. That had been enough to hold his own— although he'd had to run a couple of times, because the month wasn't up after the last fight.

Cap Hollister had been at the funeral and had sat with Mart. By then Mart had suspected that Cap Hollister helped Miss Ida out with money for his clothes and keep.

After the funeral Cap had said: "Well, Mart, you don't have to tell me folks think you're good. I've heard 'em say so. Want to stay with the preacher until school's over and then come to the ranch?"

Mart had nodded. That night he had run away. He couldn't stay in Rainbow with Miss Ida out there in the ground. Five years later he had ridden to the Lazy W corrals and hung up his saddle. He had been a man, easy, confident, with a lot of experience under his belt.

"I'll make a better hand now, if you can use me," he had told Cap. "I had to go."

"I understand," Cap had said briefly. "Thanks for writing me those cards, telling how you were doing. Pick a bunk and a riding string and start in the morning. If you're a top hand, your pay will say so."

Dot had been away at school then. Cap had married late, his wife hadn't lived long. He had sent his daughter East to school for a few years. Mart had remembered Dot Gaines as a towhead with pigtails, who came to Rainbow now and then with her father. She was younger, shy, polite. She could ride a horse, though, as well as ever.

He was a top hand at the Lazy W Ranch, and getting more of Cap's trust all the time, when Dot Gaines came home. Mart wouldn't have known her. Pigtails had turned into spun-gold hair. Her voice had a song note. She had Eastern clothes and hats, and came home to the ranch like a great lady. Everyone was proud of her.

Dot promptly put on riding clothes and rode the ranch like an old hand. She had come back a lady, but she was still Cap's girl. Everyone soon loved her, including Pete Diggers. Pete had never gotten over disliking Marty Gaines. Not long after Dot was home for good, Mart began to suspect Pete resented his being on the Lazy W, around Dot all the time. From then on things had gotten worse between them. If Dot ever suspected, she gave no sign. She liked Pete, maybe enough to marry him.

On the ride into Rainbow this morning Mart was thinking about Pete marrying Dot when Dot's chuckle brought his look to her.

"You were scowling. You looked like fighting, Mart."

Mart laughed. "Sleepy, I guess. I made a long ride yesterday."

"Dad told me." Dot was twenty-two now. She sat her cream mare easily. In riding clothes she still had the look of a great lady, and somehow the look of Cap Hollister's daughter, too. There was smiling strength in her small straight nose, in the generous firmness of her mouth. There was understanding and humor and strength in her blue eyes. Sometimes Dot's eyes squinted a little like Cap's eyes did. At such times she seemed to have Cap's shrewd grasp of all about her. "I hope Pete didn't get hurt last night," Dot said.

"I doubt if he did," Mart said casually. "Pete had twenty men in his posse. He told me only three were cornered in the mine. Four at the most."

"Pete got them, of course," Dot said. "He is a good sheriff, isn't he?"

"None better," Mart admitted honestly.

"But you don't like him," Dot teased.

"He doesn't like me."

"He's never said so. Why shouldn't he like you, Mart?"

Mart chuckled wryly. "I was the Hangtown Kid when Pete first knew me. Don't you remember?"

They'd never talked about Hangtown. "I was too little to remember," Dot said. "I know you lived in Hangtown once, Mart."

Dot looked west toward the Indian Heads. Mart wished he knew what she was thinking. Dot's face had gone sober for a moment. "Was it as bad a place as they say, Mart?"

"Pretty bad, I guess. My father sort of ran things."

"What was he like, Mart? Or don't you want to talk about it?"

Mart pushed back his hat. "I guess he was a bad one. They called him Big Jack Gaines. He was the best man at Hangtown, and that was a lot. He was never unkind to me, now that I look back. But he was strict. I was afraid of him." Mart smiled. "And I guess I loved him, too. Hangtown ways of living were all I knew. And he was my father."

"Of course you loved him," Dot said warmly. "It must have hurt when you lost him."

Mart nodded. "It was a good thing I got away from Hangtown and met your father. He made a man of me."

"No," Dot denied quickly. "It had to be in you, Mart. Whatever you were then, you are now."

Mart could feel his face getting red. He looked away, thinking about that wild ride to find Big Jack, and the way he had cheated the posse from taking prisoners. Big Jack and Otie White deserved arrest. Both men probably deserved hanging. Mart Gaines had turned them loose again. Mart Gaines had stepped over the line, away from the law.

"Did I say something wrong?" Dot asked. "You . . . you look queer."

Mart chuckled and lied. It was the first time he had lied to Dot or anyone else that he could remember. Miss Ida had been strict about telling the truth. Mart had never liked the idea of lying, anyway, even in the Hangtown days. "I was thinking about Lobey Walters and his steers," Mart said lamely. "Something tells me Lobey is set to skin you."

"He's welcome to try," Dot said cheerfully. She lifted her quirt. "I'll race you to Twin Rocks."

Dot won the two-mile race to Twin Rocks. Her cream mare was one of the fastest horses on the range. They were still laughing as they rode into Rainbow.

The posse was back. When Pete Diggers stepped off the plank walk and Dot reined her horse over to speak with him, Mart sided her without expression. But he could feel the tightening wariness. Suddenly between him and Pete Diggers was much more than dislike. Big Jack was between them. The law was between them. It was like being the Hangtown Kid all over again.

Pete looked like he had just returned to Rainbow. Bluish

stubble made Pete's face look rough and grim. He was tired, eyes bloodshot, hair rumpled and damp with sweat at the forehead line when he took off his high-crowned hat. But Pete's smile was quick and warm and eager for Dot.

"I'd like to think you rode to town to welcome me back," Pete suggested lightly to Dot. He barely noticed Mart with a nod.

"It was steers, not sheriffs that brought me in." Dot laughed. "But we were talking about you, Pete. I was a little worried. Mart said you were safe enough, but your manhunt did sound dangerous."

"I'm glad to hear Mart thought I was safe enough," Pete said. He looked past Dot's horse to Mart. The smile was not in Pete's bloodshot eyes. But something else was in the eyes. Something deep in Pete, stirring, thinking, and it was not pleasant.

Dot must have noticed it. Mart saw teeth catch her lower lip. Her smiling eyes squinted a trifle, like Cap's eyes did when he was intent. "Did you have to kill any of the men before you got them?" she asked.

"Why, no. They all got away," Pete said. He was watching Mart.

"Dad said if you had them cornered in the mine, you'd get them," Dot said. "He told me there was only one entrance to that old mine. Anyone caught inside would be trapped."

"There was a way out," Pete said. "One of the drifts broke out into a rock chute on the west side of the mountain. We found it. A man who didn't know the mine or Hangtown would never know it was there. Most men wouldn't try to get out that way if they did know. These men did." Pete's tired face hardened. "They got out and took two of our horses while we were watching the tunnel entrance. Dan Taylor was with the horses. We found Dan at daylight, stretched cold, with his head cracked. Doc Rowntree is with Dan now. He says Dan may live, with a lot of luck."

"Oh, that's bad!" Dot exclaimed under her breath. "I'll have to see Dan's wife. Poor thing."

"Did you trail the two horses?" Mart asked. He was surprised at his calmness. It was like another man speaking.

"No trail," Pete said. The deep and thoughtful look was still in his glance. He said: "They were slick." And he added: "I'm not through with them." Pete drew a breath. "Dot, if you're going to see Dan's wife now, I'll go with you."

"Later," Dot said. "I must see Mister Walters first."

"Later," Pete agreed. His look went back to Mart as he said it. Pete's smile had a faint twist, almost ugly with some silent thought he had.

Mart remembered that faint smile, even while he was listening to Lobey Walters dicker with Dot about the steers Lobey had for sale. He was thinking about Pete, and Big Jack and Otie White, while he went about Rainbow on other business for the ranch, and while Dot called on Dan Taylor's wife with Pete Diggers. Rainbow didn't seem the same. Men greeted Mart Gaines as usual. Most of them were friends. Dan Taylor had been a friend, too.

Men who had been with the posse were still talking about the running fight that had started in the Double Loop pasture. In the Martingale Bar, Hen Magee, the blacksmith, spoke his mind to a group that included Mart.

"I remember when Hangtown was in its prime," Hen Magee observed in his deep, deliberate voice. "An honest man never knew what'd happen to him or his stock." He released his whiskey glass and thumped a big fist hard on the damp bar for emphasis. "If outlaws are moving back on Rainbow, we'd better bust it up fast."

Agreement broke out among the listeners. Mart nodded and

took half his drink. He thought that a glance or two flicked his way. Perhaps the glances had no meaning. But there were many in Rainbow who could easily recall that he had been the Hangtown Kid.

Duz Wilkerson walked in with his arm in a new cloth sling. Pete Diggers came with Duz. They had been talking, and they had the intent look of men with knowledge between them. Mart's first impulse was to finish his drink and walk out. But he had never run from things. He waited, impassive and guarded against the satisfied look on Pete Diggers's now clean-shaven face, and the sly air of expectation that made Duz Wilkerson look sharper than ever.

Pete's nod accepted a drink for Duz and himself from John Spencer, the gray and genial head of the bank. Along the bar were mostly substantial men in Rainbow and the ranches around. The talk continued, Pete joining in. Duz Wilkerson had a flushed look, as if excitement were keeping him on edge. Duz spoke finally. Mart guessed he had been waiting for the right moment.

"I didn't know whether I'd make it back yesterday with this arm, the way I'd lost blood. It gave me a bad moment to see Mart ahead of me. I thought at first he was one of the bandits." Duz laughed. "I wasn't looking for Mart Gaines away out there on that old Hangtown path so late in the day."

Smiling, Pete Diggers said, as if just struck by the thought: "How'd you happen to be over that way, Gaines?"

Now there were listeners interested. Mart answered readily: "I was looking for tracks."

"Cow tracks?" Pete amiably wanted to know.

"Horse tracks," Mart said mildly, aware now how Pete and Duz were hemming him in with the talk. "I thought those gunmen might have headed out that way."

"That's funny," said Pete, puzzled. "Duz Wilkerson was telling me you didn't know anything about me being out with a posse. He had to tell you about it."

"Yes," Mart agreed. The look on Pete's face was satisfied. "I didn't know you'd bother about trouble near Myrtle City," Mart said calmly. "I'd met Cady Miller riding home from Rainbow and Cady told me about the hold-up. I made a guess it might do to see if any strangers were heading toward the Ten Dog breaks. Didn't seem worthwhile to ride into Rainbow and talk about it." Mart grinned. "When I met Duz, I found out I'd made a good guess. So I went on to help out if I could."

That explained everything. Pete looked as if his loop had made a bad miss. Duz was disappointed. "You didn't say anything about Cady Miller," Duz complained.

"You were doing most of the talking," Mart reminded. "A man has to speak fast to get in a word around you, Duz."

Laughter agreed with that statement. "You even asked me what gun bunch we had a fight with," Duz said sulkily.

"I'm still wondering, Duz. What bunch was it?"

"And when I asked where you was headed, you said you was taking a short cut," Duz persisted.

"I was, to the Ten Dogs." Mart chuckled. "Curiosity keeps you worried, doesn't it, Duz?"

That raised more laughter. Hen Magee dropped his big hand on the bar again. "Duz'll poison himself someday from not knowing all that's going on. Boys, have another drink, and mind what I tell you. Rainbow better watch sharp. We'll have strangers fattening off us again."

The talk turned away from Mart. Pete looked at his watch and walked out. Pete would remember. His mind had fastened on Mart Gaines and it would stay there. Mart walked outside in a few minutes. He had not felt like this in years. He had changed inside.

Rainbow itself seemed to have changed. The same street was

sided by the same familiar buildings. More faces were in town than usual. The vague excitement in the air was understandable. But Mart had the old, uneasy feeling that he was a stranger here. He walked the street, speaking with people he knew—and he did not belong with these people. They lived on one side of the law. They lived on the right side of the law with Cap Hollister, Dot, and Pete Diggers. Mart Gaines had stepped across the line. He was back where the Hangtown Kid had been, before and after the big fight, years ago.

Dot Hollister was finally ready to leave for the ranch. Mart was silent as they rode together. Dot looked at him several times, increasingly puzzled.

"Is anything wrong, Mart?"

"Guess I'm sleepy," Mart answered. He had the quick thought that lying to Dot was getting to be a habit after last night.

"Too many drinks?" Dot suggested.

"Maybe."

"You're old enough to handle drinking," Dot said. She had never talked like this, rather soberly, with an edge of disapproval.

"I was killing time while you were with Pete."

"You could have come with us."

"Didn't want to."

"What you do is none of my business," Dot said after a moment. "I guess I was thinking of Dad. Don't you know how proud he is of you, Mart?"

"Is he?"

"You're almost like a son to him," Dot said warmly. "He wanted a boy, and he had to be satisfied with me. He . . . he rather made you his boy. Haven't you ever seen how it is?"

Mart looked at her soberly. "I know how he's treated me. Yes, I think I've guessed a lot of things that haven't been said."

"So that makes us almost brother and sister, doesn't it?" Dot laughed.

"I don't want to be a brother!" Mart protested violently before he thought.

Dot's look was startled. Color came into her face. Mart thought she was angry. He was unprepared for Dot's laugh that dismissed the matter.

"You don't have to be . . . I'll race you again." Dot was still laughing as her mare broke ahead.

Mart quirted his horse and followed. He felt worse than ever. Dot had put into blunt words all that was uneasy and worried in his thoughts. Dot and Cap would never understand about last night at Hangtown.

IV

It was an evening nine days later when Cap Hollister came in from Rainbow and took his place at the head of the supper table. Cap's leathery face was grave.

High Tack lifted an inquiring eyebrow at Mart. Dot said: "Coyotes killed a calf on the other side of Arroyo Blanco. They're getting bad again."

Cap spooned pan gravy on his potatoes before he said shortly: "Wolves are bad, too." He reached for the pepper and looked along the table. "The bank at Blue Cañon was robbed yesterday, late. Bold as brass hold-up by five strangers. They got away, riding north. Telegraph brought the news this way."

Paso Jack, a blond, cheerful top hand, said: "If they went north from Blue Cañon, Pete Diggers won't need to worry about 'em."

Blue Cañon was two days north by saddle. Cap swallowed a mouthful of food and growled: "I own a chunk of that Blue Cañon bank stock. Won't nick me much if the bank goes broke, but I don't like the signs. First the Myrtle City stage. Now Blue

Cañon. My guess is it's the same bunch."

"Only three got away from Pete's posse," Dot reminded.

"That's what I don't like," said Cap bluntly. "If it's the same bunch, they've picked up two more bad ones. Be a dozen or more before you know it. Outlaws are like buzzards . . . they smell dead meat and start gathering."

"It might be they'll keep moving north, away from here," Mart suggested slowly.

Cap looked at him, squinting a little, not smiling. Mart remembered that old feeling that Cap could look inside a man and tell what was there.

"Might be they won't," Cap said deliberately. "Those Ten Dog badlands and the Indian Heads are the best outlaw cover in three hundred miles. That bunch would be smart to head straight this way from Blue Cañon." Cap cut into his steak, hard. "I think they're smart. Look how they left Diggers and his posse flat-footed at the old Gloriosa Mine." Cap speared a cut of steak with his fork. "Dan Taylor's head is a little better, but he's still a sick man. He just missed getting killed by that crack on the head."

Cap chewed hard, scowled. Mart caught a look from Dot. It might have meant anything. Dot looked worried. Mart tried to chuckle, failed, and ate silently. He said finally: "What did the men look like?"

"Masked," said Cap shortly. "But one of them was big and gray-haired. Bound to be one of the men who stopped the Myrtle City stage."

That night Mart walked out and sat on the corral bars in the starlight, smoking. Big Jack had not changed. He'd never change while he lived. Big Jack was a bad one.

Mart took from his pocket an old, smooth-worn, whittled wooden revolver. Big Jack had cut it deftly with a sheath knife. The kid in Hangtown had been proud of the wooden weapon.

Somehow in all the years since, the wooden toy had been a link back to Big Jack. It kept fresh memories of things Big Jack had done, like any father. Things that were good to remember. When Big Jack had been gone for days, the kid would wait eagerly for his return. Like any kid waiting for his father. But Big Jack was a bad one. Cap Hollister had done more for that kid than Big Jack had ever done.

A quiet step came to the corral bars. Dot's calm voice said: "Do you want to be alone, Mart?"

"I'm tired of being alone," Mart said simply.

Dot swung up lightly and sat beside him, facing the other way. A comfortable silence fell between them.

"I think Dad's worried about that hold-up," Dot said finally. "I know it isn't the money he might lose. Something else is on his mind."

Mart built a cigarette. He took twice as long as usual. The match flame showed Dot watching him gravely. Mart held the match a moment, looking at her. He let it drop and the starlight came about them. "Feel like a sister tonight?" he asked slowly.

"If you want me to, Mart."

Mart looked at the dark shapes of horses standing at the back of the corral. "Suppose Cap helped rob that Blue Cañon bank? Would you want me to go after him?"

"He wouldn't."

"Suppose Cap was a bad one," said Mart. "The law wanted him . . . but you had some feeling for him. Would you want me to go after him? Maybe bring him to a hang rope?"

Dot sat without moving. Her hand reached out to Mart's hand. "Would you go, Mart?"

Mart sighed and held the smaller hand. "You can't tell me, can you?"

Dot shook her head. Her voice in a moment was troubled. "You're trying to tell me something, aren't you, Mart?"

"Maybe," Mart said. He put the wooden gun in Dot's fingers. "My dad whittled this for me when I was a kid in Hangtown. I was thinking about him when you came. He was a bad one . . . but he made toys for me. I . . ."—Mart swallowed—"I can't forget it."

"Don't ever forget it," Dot urged huskily.

Mart patted her hand and shoved the wooden gun inside his belt. He chuckled. "Thanks, little sister."

In the morning Cap Hollister was his usual self, gruff and profane, as he watched another day start on the Lazy W. He bellowed to Mart from the saddle shed. "Send a man over beyond Arroyo Blanco to see if the coyotes have done any more dirt."

"You go, Paso!" Mart called to Paso Jack. "I'll ride over to Bull Creek Spring early this afternoon. We'll scout around from there. Take enough rifle shells in case you see anything to shoot at."

That suited Paso Jack, who liked to hunt. Paso was also better than an Indian at following a trail. At noon Mart rode in for a fresh horse and his rifle, and Dot said: "I'll ride over to Bull Creek, too, Mart."

"I thought you would," Mart said, grinning.

They headed for Bull Creek at an easy gallop, saying little and scanning the sky for wheeling buzzards, which might mark other dead calves. Dot was the first one to sight buzzards. Her gauntleted hand pointed to the northwest sky. "Six or seven of them, Mart. You can just see them."

"We'd better meet Paso at the spring first," Mart decided. "It's nearer, and he's probably seen those buzzards and had a look."

Bull Creek Spring was a rock basin at the foot of a yellow sandstone ridge through which Bull Creek cut, on its way from the high Indian Heads. In dry months Bull Creek was a trickle, but the spring never ran out. Cap had said Bull Creek Spring was worth thirty sections of land. In drought cattle walked to the spring from more than thirty sections of range, and there was always water in the rock pool to carry them through to the rains.

Paso Jack was not at the spring. Mart pointed with his quirt handle to fresh horse sign. "We're late, I guess. Paso must have ridden out for a look at those buzzards."

They rode north from the spring. The big scavenger birds were still wheeling low.

"Paso rode there," Dot guessed. "He's keeping the birds up."

Mart nodded and scanned the distance for sign of Paso Jack on his horse. Low ridges through here, dry arroyos, scattered prickly pear beds, and clumps of cane cactus, with gnarled cedars on the higher ridges made it easy to miss a rider. Dot's cream mare was loping ahead when they topped one last ridge and started a clumsy rush of more buzzards off the ground.

"Another dead calf!" Dot called over her shoulder. And then Dot cried out something Mart did not catch. But he was near enough now to see three dead buzzards on the ground, and the body of the man who had shot them.

Paso Jack was stretched there on his back, revolver in one outflung hand. Paso's head turned slowly as the galloping horses reached him.

Paso's lips were drawn off his teeth; he seemed to be smiling. It was weakness. As Mart kneeled on one side, Dot on the other, they could see Paso struggling to breathe. His eyes had a dull, old-man look. It took an effort, but Paso managed to smile wanly.

"Been wonderin' if you'd come," Paso said weakly.

"What happened?" Mart demanded.

"Stranger shot me." Paso had to suck breath painfully again. A damp blood spot showed above his belt. He had not bled much. Mart could see where Paso had painfully crawled on the

101

slope, toward higher ground.

Dot looked at Mart. Her face was white, strained; she was close to tears.

Paso spoke in his labored weakness. "Saw a feller headin' toward Bull Creek and I cut over to ride with him. He waited down the slope there. Drawed and plugged me soon as I come up. Took my horse. Guess he thought I wouldn't last long, hit center this way. Didn't bother to finish me off."

"Ever see him before?" Mart asked.

"Nope," Paso whispered. Mart had to bend over to catch the rest of it. "Small feller . . . kinda thin face . . . pointed. . . ."

"Sort of like Duz Wilkerson in Rainbow?" Mart suggested.

Paso nodded weakly. "Knew he was like someone I'd seen. Wasn't Wilkerson. . . . I'm thirsty. . . ."

Dot said quickly: "I'll ride back to the spring and get some water. . . ."

"Ride to the ranch and get the buckboard started this way," Mart differed. "Send a man to Rainbow for Doc Rowntree. First help me get Paso on my horse. I'll be bringing him on a beeline to the ranch."

Paso was bleeding inside. Dot might not know how badly Paso was hit. Mart knew it. Paso did, too. When Dot's cream mare was a flying bit of color in the distance ahead, and Mart was carefully following with his limp and heavy burden held across knees and saddle horn with one arm, Paso said: "Waste of time. I'm all tore up inside."

"Keep quiet," Mart ordered gruffly. He wished he could gallop. He silently cursed the jarring this was giving Paso. "Doc Rowntree will fix you up."

Paso's grimace was an effort at smiling. His teeth were clenched. His eyes stayed closed and his breath came harder. "Won't hunt them coyotes now," Paso mumbled. Mart had to bend down to catch the words.

The sun was low and dark beyond the Ten Dog buttes when Paso died, his head rolling slackly against Mart's arm. The pain lines smoothed out. Paso's features seemed to sleep peacefully.

Paso had been the life of the bunkhouse, the biggest joker, and always a square-shooter. He was the kind of man Cap Hollister liked to hire. Mart rode on with his face set. Presently he saw the dust drift that marked the buckboard and riders from the ranch.

Cap himself was driving the buckboard straight across the range. Cap's prideful team of gray running horses was hitched to the buckboard. Cap was driving with slashing whip like a wild man, keeping the buckboard in the heel dust of his saddle riders.

Mart pulled up and waited. Shorty, High Tack, Old Jim, Dot were with the buckboard. They came with a rush and a swirl of dust, and Cap's profane shouts to the gray team as he sawed to a stop and sprang to the ground.

"How is he?" Cap called.

Mart let them take his inert burden. He climbed stiffly down and helped lift Paso into the buckboard.

Cap's wrinkled, leathery face was bitter. Hard and set, too. Mart had never seen Cap look quite like this in any anger of Cap's he had witnessed.

"It was murder," Cap said in a rasping monotone. "Dot told me what Paso said. Murder."

"Yes," Mart agreed. Then he said, "Shorty, your roan is in better shape than my horse. Swap you."

"What are you gonna do?" Cap snapped.

"Ride out," Mart told him mildly.

"We'll all go as soon as Pete Diggers gets to the ranch with some men. I sent word for Pete to come."

"Good idea," Mart stated, nodding. He swung on Shorty's roan and pushed his rifle into the scabbard.

"You wait for the sheriff!" Cap ordered loudly.

"I've waited long enough," Mart said.

"You'll get shot, too, trailing that killer alone!"

"I've got it to do," Mart said. He looked at Dot as he reined around. Dot kneed her horse to him.

"Let Pete do it, Mart." And Dot said for him alone: "You know who you're going after, don't you?"

"I know who I might find," Mart told her. His face felt frozen. He said harshly: "It doesn't matter. Paso was my friend. Cap may be the next one. I did my duty and more, once . . . now I'll pay for the chance."

His quirt drove the roan off fast. Mart did not look back. He had gone half a mile when Cap Hollister ranged beside him. High Tack and Shorty were with Cap.

"You darn' fool!" Cap bellowed. And then Cap, riding close, called: "You think I seen you grow from a hot-headed button to a real man so's Hangtown can take you away? I'll kill that four-fingered horse thief myself, like I thought I'd done years ago!"

Cap knew. Cap must have known all along who had helped Big Jack get away from Pete's posse. Cap could look down inside a man and tell what was there. A numb and frozen feeling inside Mart broke. Cap was siding him like a father in what lay ahead. For the first time Mart knew what it was like to feel that the Hangtown Kid was another person. Not Mart Gaines.

That was all they said about it. From then on in the fading afternoon they were four men on a manhunt. High Tack and Shorty knew only that the stranger ahead had shot Paso Jack. If the trail led to the bandits who had robbed the Blue Cañon bank, so much the better. Mart wondered what the two top hands would think if they knew he was riding toward his real father.

They found where Paso had been shot out of the saddle. Paso's horse had been led toward Bull Creek Spring. From the spring, the tracks headed across the back range toward the Indian Heads.

Cap squinted at the somber mountain crests outlined against the last gory light of day. "Can't follow these tracks much longer," he announced regretfully. "After dark, a cavalry regiment couldn't spread out and find anything in them mountains."

"I've been thinking," Mart said. "Maybe I know something that will help." He reined to a walk, staring at the upthrust of the mountains ahead. He asked Cap, who was close on his left: "Did you ever hear of a cañon somewhere north of Hangtown called Snake Cañon?" Mart added: "Haven't thought of the name since I was a kid."

Cap gave him a sharp, squinty look. "Was there any Indians or Mexicans around Hangtown when you were there?"

"There was an old Apache, who stayed drunk most of the time." Mart smiled at the memory. "They called him Drinks Plenty. He knew every trail in the Indian Heads, I guess. I remember him drawing trails on the ground with a stick in front of our cabin. He seemed to be teaching Big Jack all about the mountains."

Cap nodded. "You heard talk of Snake Cañon, huh?"

"It was supposed to be a place to light out to if a man couldn't make Hangtown," Mart said. "Maybe I dreamed it, but I seem to remember talk one night about not taking rustled cattle into Snake Cañon, or leaving any kind of a trail into the cañon."

"You didn't dream it," Cap said slowly. "I knew an old Mexican who was part Apache. He'd lived out like a buck with 'em in his young days. Killed his share of settlers, I always thought. He told me about Snake Cañon. Called it Culebra. Cañon Culebra. It was the old Apache way into the Indian Heads." Cap smiled thinly. "It's called Crooked Cañon now."

Mart looked his astonishment. His smile was thin, too. "I've been up Crooked Cañon. Now I'll back my guess. Hangtown's not healthy any more. The Ten Dog *malpais* will be dry-camping this time of year. Somewhere up above the first waterfall in Crooked Cañon is the camp we want."

"Wouldn't be surprised," Cap agreed.

"There's a moon tonight."

"More light to shoot any man who follows tracks into the cañon," Cap said dryly.

Shorty broke in: "There's dust 'way back there toward Bull Creek. Coming this way, I think."

They all wheeled to a stop, scanning back. The land fell away in a vast sweep of distance, until the haze and the coming night met at the far horizon. The high clouds were still bright with light and color. And far toward Bull Creek a low drift of dust might have been lifted by a swirling wind. But there was not enough wind to lift dust. The quiet of coming twilight was over Rainbow range. While they looked, the dust drift moved perceptibly.

"Horses. Plenty of 'em," Cap guessed. "Mart, you got better eyes than I have. Ain't it horses?"

"A good bunch," Mart assented. "I'll guess it's Pete Diggers's posse. He rode straight for Bull Creek Spring and turned this way. They're burning leather to get over the trail and catch us before dark."

"Good," Cap grunted. "We'll wait."

"Best thing to do. I'll ride on."

"Now wait!" Cap protested.

"I'd rather go into Crooked Cañon ahead of Pete Diggers." Mart shook up his horse as Cap started to protest again. He looked back and saw Shorty spurring toward the posse, but Cap and High Tack were following him. And because there was no way to lose the two men, Mart eased the pace.

Cap said nothing once they were riding together again. His

wrinkled face was set with purpose. He was chewing tobacco vigorously. Mart was leading now. He left the tracks they had been following, and pointed the roan horse straight for Crooked Cañon. Darkness came over them in the high foothills, where cedar and pine thrust up and the first rock cliffs were bold outcrops of the mightier masses ahead. Moonrise was a full hour away, but there was starlight in the new dark.

Cap said: "If a look-out spotted the posse dust, we're wasting time."

High Tack said: "Might be wasting time anyway. This is a guessing ride."

Mart rode without talking. The upflung mountain masses were holding his thoughts on Big Jack. He felt no bitterness now. Always he had known what Big Jack was. And anyway, it was Otie White who had shot Paso Jack and left him to die. He wanted to think, and he did think, that Big Jack Gaines would not have shot Paso down in cold blood. But Big Jack had brought Otie White back to Rainbow country. Big Jack would be giving the orders and have the reasons for returning. They would be bold and shrewd reasons. Big Jack was no coyote who skulked and ran. He was a lobo wolf, clever and without fear. But a wolf pack always had a weak one who would snap up poison bait or spring a trap, if the old he-wolf was not close. Otie White had done something like that when he shot Paso Jack.

Cap Hollister spoke, as if he were reading Mart's thoughts again. "Wouldn't be many outlaws smart enough to head right back into country where a posse jumped them not long before." And a few minutes later Cap said: "We better wait for moonrise, hadn't we? I ain't sure just where we are."

"Wait here," Mart said. "I'll take a look around."

He reined back hard and drove in spurs, and was away from Cap's protest and out of sight in a moment. He had guessed

Cap was a little confused in the dark, and he had waited for the moment to get off by himself. Now, riding hard and recklessly, he swung the roan on a zigzag course through the rock outcrops and the sharp ridges. He stopped to listen once, and he was alone on the blowing horse. Mart thought he knew where he was, and he went on.

Crooked Cañon broke out of the mountains like a knife gash through five hundred feet of solid rock. The water came down a rock trough in the middle of the gash. A man could jump across, or be over his knees in the middle. And when the great snows melted on the peaks or the heavy rains came, the flood torrent was deep between the rock walls. One never knew when water might come rushing down to trap the unwary who ventured into the ravine. For that reason few men on Rainbow range knew a great deal about Crooked Cañon.

V

The moon was just under the horizon when Mart reached the bottom water. He was at the foot of a rock cliff that towered dizzily toward the stars. The black slit of Crooked Cañon looked even narrower than it was, ominous, forbidding.

The roan horse drank. Mart went flat and drank, too. Only in freshets did the cold current run far from the cañon mouth. The water vanished in the sands of the lower channel. No one had ever found where it came up again.

Mart rode into the current and turned upstream. The blackness about him became absolute. The fast water tugged at the roan's legs. A constant tumbling murmur beat against the cañon walls, and funneled up and up, so that the high sky seemed to be whispering, also. The sky was a faint band of pale stars that appeared to roof his private night. He had the feeling that the mountain was closing in above, about to crush anything that moved on the cañon floor.

The roan advanced carefully, snorting now and then with disapproval. Presently the cañon began to bend a little to the right. Mart heard the current rushing against the rock at his left. The scouring action had worn away the rock, making the channel wider. Mart put the horse to the right. The water was quickly shallow, and the roan climbed out on dry footing.

Here was the spot where one could tell whether others had recently passed up the cañon. Mart dismounted. He listened intently. The gurgle and rush of the current were all he could hear. He bent over with a match. A flick of his thumbnail brought the end flaring. The cupped and wavering glow struck down on the dark rock underfoot. There, glistening slightly, were the wet marks left by someone who had preceded him.

Mart flipped the match into the water. He carefully tightened the saddle cinches. When he swung up, he pulled the rifle from the scabbard and levered a shell into the chamber. He made sure that the revolver was ready. Any step from this point on might meet a waiting gun. Paso Jack's body was proof enough that strangers in Crooked Cañon would get short welcome.

Mart thought of many things as he advanced—of Pete Diggers's posse, of Cap Hollister and High Tack—but behind all that was the image of Big Jack, somewhere ahead on the mountain. Big Jack, the bad one—who had whittled a wooden gun. Big Jack and the outlaws who took his orders, as dangerous now to peaceful ranchers as the Apaches who used to snake down this cañon for the blood hunt over the grasslands. It should have been called Dead Man's Cañon. Men would probably die tonight. Mart wished he could turn back. But he had not turned back at Hangtown the other night, and he could not now.

Mart had the queer feeling that Paso Jack was riding with him now. Cap Hollister and Dot were riding with him, too. And Miss Ida. All those friends of Rainbow range who respected

Mart Gaines, of the Lazy W, were riding right with him. The rocky shelf beside the current lifted in an almost impassable way past the first waterfall, and went on. At times the roan horse had to go back in the current for short distances. There were other falls, other sharp uplifts in the rough trail. Always, in the blackness ahead, lay the threat of outlaw guns.

The sky far above was brighter with moonlight. Looking up, Mart could see trees clinging precariously to the high rocks. Overhanging masses of the cañon wall looked ready to thunder down, as had their predecessors fallen in the past. The trail went over great heaps of fallen rock. Some slides had evidently blocked the cañon for long periods. Water poured between great boulders at those points with strange and restless sounds. It was like the cañon itself talking, whispering, moaning about the dead years and the memories.

Big Jack had known what he was doing when he came back here from the Blue Cañon robbery. Threat hung in the cañon, and was worse because of what had to be done ahead. Mart reached the first good camp spot without any warning but another bend in the cañon.

The horse lifted its head quickly. The taint of wood smoke reached through the night. Mart dismounted fast, his finger at the rifle trigger, then leading the roan. The singing current covered minor sounds. There was enough starlight above to see how the cañon widened here. A shelf-like flat with trees and stunted bushes, two acres at the most—at the back, rocks went steeply up, until far above they lifted sheer again for a hundred feet. A man could climb to that last hundred feet. No more. To escape, he would have to go up or down the cañon. He could not climb out.

An old pole cabin had been built back in the trees, perhaps in the riotous days of Hangtown. Big Jack might have ordered it built. Years ago when Mart had come this way, idly exploring

Crooked Cañon, the cabin had long been deserted. From where Mart stood now the cabin was invisible. He could still smell the wood coals smoldering inside. Somewhere back in the trees a horse nickered. Mart barely stopped the roan from answering.

There should be a guard, perhaps close to him. He led the roan forward a step, and then another step, searching the night, listening. A match flared among the first trees. A cupped hand held the light to a smoke. That would be the guard. Mart went on, until the cañon narrowed again. He was still on the trail. Any man who tried to escape up the cañon would have to pass right close to him.

Mart left the roan there, ground-tied, not caring much whether it moved or not. By now the posse would be moving in from below, and he had the uptrail blocked. The water noises covered the slight sounds of his advance toward the guard. Still the moon had not pushed light into the cañon. The long file of armed riders would be feeling their way through the cañon blackness. Haste prodded Mart. He had to do this alone.

The cigarette end sparked once as it was dropped and stepped on. Mart melted into the scrubby bushes and came at the guard from behind. He found the dark blob of a figure half seated on a large boulder. Looking at the deep shadows downslope, Mart could see how he had passed without notice. The guard should have been on the trail, where the shelf-like space began. Strangers evidently were not expected tonight.

The guard lifted his arms and yawned. He held a rifle. Mart stepped to his shoulder, unnoticed, and then some animal sense must have warned the man. He turned.

"Just reach," Mart ordered bruskly. He prodded hard with the Colt muzzle, and the man shrank away and hurriedly thrust both arms and the rifle high overhead.

Mart took the rifle and tossed it away. He found two guns in the guard's side holsters, and thrust them inside his belt.

"How many in the cabin?" Mart questioned.

The man hesitated before answering sullenly: "Three."

"Otie White, too?"

"Who are you?"

"Doesn't matter. Is Big Jack Gaines in there, too?"

"I ain't talkin'."

"Walk easy," Mart ordered, prodding with the gun. "No noise."

They came to the old cabin that way. Quiet voices were talking inside. A thread of dim light showed at the door edge. Rusty hinges creaked as the guard opened the door and shouldered in, hands still up at shoulder level.

Mart followed at his heels, and stepped fast to the left, and put his back against the cabin wall. "Don't move!" he ordered. He saw the faces and added: "Warn them, Big Jack!"

They were four, instead of three, sitting cross-legged around a red and blue saddle blanket of Navajo weave. They had been playing cards by light of a candle thrust in an empty whiskey bottle. The chips were gold coins, and by the number of them on the saddle blanket, Mart guessed the Blue Cañon Bank was banking the game.

Big Jack was facing the door. Otie White was opposite, with his back to the door. The other two men were strangers, and so was the guard. They all had stubble beards; they had the look of men who had been traveling long and hard. They all looked older than Mart, but Big Jack was the only gray-haired one. Five of them—the five who had visited Blue Cañon. By their frozen attitudes, Mart guessed they were waiting for a move. Big Jack was the only one who smiled; in the wavering candle glow his deeply lined, long face with its white mustache warmed to some inner humor.

"Marty," Big Jack said, "you don't need to hold a gun on me."

"On you, too," Mart differed. It was like addressing a stranger. Thought of Paso Jack made them all strangers. "I told you to move on off my range," Mart said. He added with a sudden harshness in his throat: "It's the only thing I ever really asked you."

"This ain't your range, Marty. We're just stopping here."

"After Blue Cañon," Mart said.

Big Jack did not deny it. He chuckled softly. He had not put his hands up, and he reached forward and lifted a stack of yellow gold pieces, and let them clink down from his fingertips. "Blue Cañon ain't Rainbow," he said. "I had it planned to meet these other boys near Blue Cañon, and we did." Big Jack clinked the gold again. "This is a good place to rest, Marty, until we get on to other things. That Myrtle City bank has a lesson coming. Next time we'll get gold instead of lead from their stage shipment."

"You know there'll be no next time," Mart said coldly. "Blue Cañon, Myrtle City, Rainbow . . . it's all the same to me. I got you away from the law once, and told you to let me live my way. You almost killed a man getting those two horses. A friend of mine. I've had to look his wife in the eye and lie."

"We had to have horses . . . and there he was before we knowed it, Marty."

"The sheriff suspects I helped you out of Hangtown. I grew up with him. He's never forgotten I was the Hangtown Kid. Damn you," Mart said thickly. "All you ever brought me was misery."

Big Jack shrugged. "I didn't mean to, kid."

The broad-shouldered man at Big Jack's left growled: "Are we gonna sit here and jaw with him all night?"

"Shut up," Big Jack said. "I'll do the talking, Ben. It's been a long time since I've seen my kid. I like to hear his voice."

"I played straight with you," Mart said. "And you had to

bring this pack of killers back where I live, and start killing off my own men." Mart swallowed. "I always thought of you as the Old Man, who used to bring me something when you rode back to Hangtown. Now, when I think of you, I'll be seeing Paso Jack, one of my men on the ranch, dying as I tried to get him to a doctor this afternoon."

Big Jack looked across the stacked gold on the blanket. "Otie, you didn't tell me you killed a man to get that horse."

"He was comin' at me." Otie shifted nervously, his hands up to shoulder height. "He'd have pulled a gun quick."

"Paso told me before he died . . . it was murder. He wasn't even looking for trouble," Mart said with flat and heavy harshness.

Big Jack seemed to shake his hand. It was a small movement, almost too fast to see in the dim light. The tiny, double-barreled vest gun was barely visible in Big Jack's hand, but the solid jar of the shot filled the pole cabin.

Otie White yelled with the report, and then he caved back toward Mart's feet, and one blank eye socket was bleeding. Mart could not have stopped it if he had shot at Big Jack.

"Otie ain't going anywhere," Big Jack said. His mouth was a hard and vicious line under the white mustache. "Otie knew better than to kill a man on Rainbow, let alone the Lazy W."

The man called Ben suddenly said: "Listen! Guns!"

"Hold still!" Mart told them. "That's the posse coming. You'll have your chance with the law."

Ben began to swear. "Your own kid sending you in to be hanged, Jack! You going to stand for it?"

"Why, no," Big Jack said. "He won't shoot me, either. Bet you, he won't."

"Sit down, Pop!" Mart called. His voice shook.

Big Jack stood up. He was smiling a little. "Marty," he said, "you were always a good kid. But you know I always meant what I said. You ain't gonna hang me."

"Sit down!" Mart warned desperately.

He had come here a man, to do what had to be done. He thumbed back the gun hammer—and suddenly he couldn't do it. Not to that tall, slightly smiling old man. Any of the others, yes—but not that one. And the others were sitting in taut expectancy, watching Big Jack.

The Derringer's report filled the cabin again. Mart looked down dumbly at his empty gun hand. The big Colt had dropped from numb fingers. The bullet had torn his arm above the wrist. Blood was welling out. Big Jack was on him, cat-like, as he looked, crowding him against the wall, jerking the revolvers from inside his belt.

"Get going, you fools!" Big Jack yelled. "I'll handle him!"

Mart lunged, taking Big Jack with him. He heard a man shout outside. "What's the matter in there? The law's coming!" Then Big Jack hit him with a gun barrel.

Mart came awake with blackness around him. He struggled and he was tied. Saddle rope had his ankles and knees drawn back and tied to his arms, lashed behind his back. He was on the hard dirt floor of the cabin. The dim red coals of the fireplace were close. The night outside was full of gunfire. Bullets were driving into the cabin wall, slashing through the door. A fast burst of shots roared out inside the cabin. In ears deafened by the sound Mart heard his name called.

"Marty! Can you hear me?"

"Big Jack?"

"Sure, kid." The candle was out, but Big Jack was beside him a moment later. "I figured you'd come out of it pretty quick. That arm's got a tie around the bullet hole. It'll be all right."

"Where're the other men?"

"They got a little start up the cañon. Maybe they'll make it. I

115

had another man down on the flats watching. I guess you slipped by him. He shot at the posse all the way up the cañon and held 'em back some." Big Jack chuckled. "I didn't make it. Looks like I'm cornered here."

"You asked for it," Mart mumbled.

"Sure I did. This ain't the first time I've been cornered."

The firing died away. Mart recognized Pete Diggers's voice shouting: "Come out of there, if you can walk! We're all around you! Gaines, that goes for you, too!"

Big Jack moved quickly. He emptied another handgun in a tearing crescendo of shots, and was back again, hugging the floor, chuckling as the posse guns raked the cabin once more.

"Got some moon outside now," Big Jack said. "You know, Marty, you'd have felt real bad if you'd kept me to hang. I was sure of it when you couldn't shoot me." Big Jack was reloading as he talked. "That sheriff is real nasty about you. He thinks you're shooting, too. Be a surprise when he finds you like this." And then Big Jack said: "So you've still got that old wood gun I whittled for you. Makes me feel good, kid. You kinda liked the old man, didn't you?"

"Any kid feels that way."

"I guess so," Big Jack said. "So long, kid. I was sort of waiting until you could talk. Now I'll make a run for it."

"You won't make it in the moonlight," Mart said.

"It'll save you watching me hanged," Big Jack said, laughing softly. "I never was much good, I guess, but you keep that wood gun just the same. I'm sorry Otie played the fool like he did. He always was a gun-crazy killer. *Adiós.*"

The door opened, slammed shut. Outside, the guns crashed louder. Then they fell silent, waiting.

Pete Diggers shouted: "Come out, Mart Gaines!"

"Come in and untie me!" Mart called.

Cap Hollister was the one who slashed the saddle rope and

helped Mart up. Cap had been swearing. He wheeled on Pete Diggers in the candlelight.

"Told you not to make a fool of yourself, Diggers! Does this look like Mart helped them killers?" Cap snorted. "Mart tried to do your job for you, and didn't quite make it!"

Men were holding lit candles over the body of Otie White.

"He's the one who shot Paso Jack," Mart told them, and he asked slowly: "What happened to the last man out of here?"

Cap answered quickly: "He must have been hit bad before he stepped out. He just stood there in the moonlight. Couldn't have missed him." Cap turned his head and spat. "He's a stranger. Never seen him before. Ain't that right, Mart?"

Cap knew. He was trying to cover up. Mart stood there with the bloody bandanna tied above his wrist. He looked at their faces; they would believe what he said.

"He was Big Jack Gaines," Mart said slowly. A smile came with it, and no bitterness now for all the memories that would link to this night. "Big Jack wasn't hurt when he walked out. He could have made a break with the others . . . but he stayed here with me." Mart took a breath. "Big Jack knew what he was doing when he stepped out there in the moonlight."

"Well, what was he doing?" Pete challenged him.

Mart searched for a reply that would tell it, and then the thing he said only made sense to him. "I guess Big Jack would call it whittling another wooden gun," he said reflectively. "One that won't ever get lost."

"Maybe you know what you're saying," Pete remarked disagreeably.

Cap swore again. "I know what he's saying and I believe it. Mart's a better man than he ever thought he was. Let's get back to the ranch, Mart. Dot's worried about us."

They were outside, at the horses, when Mart said: "Dot's worried like a sister, I guess."

"Sister?" said Cap. "What kind of fool talk is that?"

"I'll ask Dot," Mart said. "Hurry up, Cap. It's a long ride and I've got to know."

"You hurry," said Cap comfortably. "I know."

★ ★ ★ ★ ★

THE QUICKEST DRAW

★ ★ ★ ★ ★

This story marked T.T. Flynn's second appearance in Street & Smith's *Western Story Magazine* in the issue dated December 10, 1938. The editor, Jack Burr, remarked in his editorial column, "The Roundup", in the issue dated April 4, 1939 that "since the publication of the December 10th issue [in which "The Quickest Draw" first appeared] . . . we've had so many inquiries concerning the author of this yarn, which made such an outstanding hit, that we decided to find out a bit more about him." An author's portrait followed, introducing Flynn to the magazine's readers. It should be mentioned that "The Quickest Draw" is also available in a full-cast dramatization with music and sound effects in Great American Westerns: Volume Two from Graphic Audio.

I

Pres Morehead came home from his Argentine ranches on the 10:20 a.m. train, and no one in the crowd around the weathered little Cottonwood Springs station recognized the tall man in the expensive gray suit and hat whose tanned face was alert and eager with anticipation. Holding his cowhide bag, Pres Morehead stood there on the platform, putting names to faces, names he'd remembered for eleven years. And suddenly it struck him that it wasn't like what he had thought it would be.

Those two weather-beaten cow waddies sitting on the baggage truck must be Sandy Stevens and Jerry, still down for $40 a month and found on some ranch payroll. That listless man piling express packages on another truck was Bat-Ear Johnson. You couldn't mistake those ears. The brisk-looking *hombre,* fat around the middle, diamond ring on a pudgy finger, who brushed by to get on the train had to be Jonas Ridgway whose father had been president of the bank. It looked like Jonas headed the bank now, fat and easy off his loans and discounts.

¡Madre de Dios! Pres thought with dismay as he glimpsed a portly young woman holding a candy-smeared baby—Martha Peters. Something hungry and eager that had lasted through the years caused Pres Morehead to draw back into himself, and he spoke to none of them.

The hotel seemed peopled with strangers. On a whim, Pres signed the register as John Emory. Time enough to make himself known after he'd seen Tom Morehead and Phil Morehead, his father and brother. At eighteen Pres Morehead had been a ranch kid who had taken it on the run after a minor shooting scrape over a dance. Not bad trouble. His father could have easily settled it for him. But there had been other brawls, and Tom Morehead had been increasingly exasperated. And, anyway, the great horizons had been calling to restless youth.

Now, at twenty-nine, Pres Morehead rode a livery horse toward the Bar Z just as he had once left home, in riding boots and overall trousers he had changed into in his hotel room. Later there would be time enough to tell about those square miles of Argentine grassland, herds of fat cattle, the great *hacienda* that he had shared with a partner.

You could reach the Bar Z by the long pass around to Turquoise Creek, or you could take the shorter cut up Bearhead Cañon, up the narrow switchback trail over the cañon rim, and down through the steep balsam and pine slopes to the head of Turquoise Creek. Pres Morehead rode up Bearhead Cañon as he had many times in the past. A thousand feet deep, Bearhead Cañon slashed down from the mountains, and the trail up the side had dangerous caved-in spots. Twice Pres dismounted, testing the trail himself. His movements sent pebbles plunging hundreds of feet into space. Near the top the trail edge caved without warning. One hoof of the claybank flew off into space. The horse plunged forward, scrambling madly to safety. When it was over, Pres rested in the saddle, eyeing the sheer drop to the boiling current of Bear Creek, far below.

"Close," Pres said aloud, and grinned ruefully as he shook his head. The vast flat Argentine pampas got you out of the habit of this sort of thing. Pines and fir clung to the cañon walls, and the high air had a heady bite. The years rolled away, and Pres Morehead was eighteen again, whistling lightly through his teeth as he rode over the rim of Bearhead Cañon and down through the green mountain grass and trees of the long northern slope. This was Bar Z land, from the rim of Bearhead Cañon to the foothill flats far beyond Turquoise Creek. Old Tom Morehead had homesteaded on Turquoise Creek and leased and bought until he had the Bar Z as he wanted it—summer pasture on the high slopes, winter grass in the lower lands—not a big ranch but a good ranch.

Pres Morehead's eyes softened as he thought of the gruff-voiced, bull-headed old cowman who was his father. They'd never exchanged much affection, but it had been understood. It would be there, Pres knew, when he rode in after eleven years. Down into the cedars above the grassy flats of Turquoise Creek Pres rode at a lope. None of the details had changed. The picture was the same. Here was what he had hungered for in the years of exile.

The sudden, whip-like scream of a bullet, the shock as it tore the pommel leather off, was no part of that picture. Pres reined sharply. Someone had shot at him with a rifle—someone on the Bar Z. He could think of no possible explanation for such attack. The gunman came galloping through the cedars, and Pres watched with narrowing eyes. This wasn't Phil, his older brother, or old Tom Morehead, or any man he knew. A saddle scabbard showed that the stranger's repeating rifle traveled with him. Crossed cartridge belts supported business-like gun holsters. The man wore chaps and a weather-beaten old hat. In the early twenties he had a hard, young roughness that held no welcome.

"Maybe that gun went off by mistake," Pres suggested curtly.

"How come you're on Bar Z land?" the gunman questioned brusquely, studying Pres with cold, inscrutable eyes.

"You a Bar Z rider?"

"You hit it."

Pres smiled faintly. He'd met a hundred such young men, tough, hard, whose guns were for sale to handle any trouble if the pay was right. "Must be something wrong," he guessed aloud. "The Bar Z didn't used to need gunhands."

"They're riding now." The young gunman had been looking beyond Pres suspiciously. "Anyone with you?" he demanded harshly.

Pres was beginning to enjoy the situation. "I didn't see anyone," he answered gravely.

"Where'd you come from?"

"Up Bearhead Cañon from Cottonwood Springs. I'd like to visit the Bar Z, if there's no objection."

"Got business there?"

"You might say so."

"Know how to get to the ranch house?"

"I'll take a chance on finding it."

The rifle motioned him on. "The ranch house, stranger. No place else."

Funny when you thought about it—this welcome cold as a winter norther off the high peaks—but the brusque efficiency of the young gunman was sobering. Pres knew his father wouldn't hire such men if the provocation weren't great. He took the down slopes at an easy gallop, the young gunman close behind him.

They came to Turquoise Creek, far down, where the cotton-woods were tall, and Pres pointed the way to the wide draw off Turquoise Creek where the corrals, windmills, and ranch build-ings brought the past flooding back in his mind. There in the afternoon sunshine was the log-and-stone ranch house. There, too, in the warm sun was a girl, galloping past an outer corral to meet him. Pres pulled to a walk, eyeing her in half consterna-tion. She wore overall trousers, riding boots, a loose, free blouse. Her hat hung to the saddle pommel, and her brown hair was free in the wind. Her voice, clear and young, had a ring of authority as she called to the young gunman.

"What is it, McAlister?"

There had been no women on the Bar Z. Phil Morehead must have married, and well and luckily, Pres thought. This girl had a tense, proud face and a fire of energy that came from the spirit.

Behind Pres the young gunman replied: "Found him alone this side of Bearhead Cañon. Says he came up the cañon from Cottonwood Springs, heading here to the ranch house. So I brought him in."

The girl stopped a horse's length away. Pres noted her dark eyes, warily questioning. He smiled, but there was no answering smile for him. Her saddle carried a scabbard and rifle, her belt holster a pearl-handled gun. Her voice was cool when she spoke again. "I don't know you. What do you want on Bar Z land?"

Pres gave her a broader smile. "I just dropped in to talk to Tom Morehead and Phil. You might let 'em know they've got a visitor."

Now the antagonism leaped from her, puzzling but open and direct. "Do you live around here?" she asked coldly.

"Not now," said Pres, "I used to. When I got into Cotton-wood Springs today, I rode over for a talk."

"You've had the ride for nothing," she said clearly. "My brother and I own the Bar Z now. We bought the ranch from Tom Morehead."

"I hadn't heard," Pres said slowly. "Where can I find the Morehead men, ma'am?"

At the question he would have sworn that an additional barrier came up between them, that the fire inside her flamed and defied him. "You won't find them," she said. "They're dead."

The wild, roistering years young Pres Morehead had put in on the hot, feverish lands of South America had brought iron control, but he felt the shock of that cold announcement slow his heart, and for a moment he was frozen. Then he found his voice, and surprisingly he could still speak calmly. "I hadn't heard that, either. No. It's news, ma'am. A surprise."

The girl said nothing. She sat stiffly in the saddle, watching him. After a moment she reached into a trousers pocket and brought out a gumdrop. She bit the gumdrop in two and chewed it slowly, her eyes still on him. For some reason that bit of candy fired cold anger under Pres's sudden grief. The two dead Morehead men didn't seem to bother her in the least. She was indifferent and coldly antagonistic.

"How did they die?" Pres asked evenly.

"Phil Morehead was killed in a gunfight last year. His father was shot by someone shortly after he sold the ranch. The sheriff has made no arrests in either case."

Now there was no doubt of her unfriendliness. Pres nodded impassively. "I'll ride back to Cottonwood Springs. Sorry, ma'am, that I bothered your gunman."

"They're hired to watch," she said briefly. "You're not the first. The Bar Z is closed to strangers."

She put the other half of the gumdrop into her mouth. Pres Morehead wheeled his horse with unnecessary violence and rode away without a civil parting.

II

The livery stable man was named Bratley, and his voice rasped in the thickening twilight inside the barn. "Never mind about that busted pommel. It don't matter. But who shot at you does. How'd it happen?"

"A gunman on the Bar Z gave me a stranger's welcome," Pres explained briefly.

"Might have known!" Bratley said violently. "Those damn' *Californios*! It's a wonder you didn't get a bullet in the back like old Tom Morehead did!"

Pres's hands froze on the cinch strap. His voice was brittle as he asked: "These people on the Bar Z shot Tom Morehead?"

Bratley evidently realized he had spoken out of turn. He spat and asked gruffly: "How'd you happen to be on the Bar Z?"

Pres pulled the cinch strap out of the ring. His answer was curt. "I used to know the Moreheads. Hadn't heard they weren't around here any more and rode over to the ranch to see them."

The liveryman snorted. "If you'd said something, I could have told you it was a waste of time." He paused. "Did you know 'em well?" he asked shrewdly.

"Hadn't seen 'em in years," Pres managed carelessly. "These people on the ranch have some quarrel with Tom Morehead?"

"Can't tell you," said Bratley. "You hear things. Folks talk sometimes when they ain't sure what they're saying. I never paid much attention. Guess there ain't anything I can tell you. Going to be riding out tomorrow?"

"I don't know," said Pres, and walked out.

The town hadn't changed much—the same dusty main street, a few new buildings with false fronts. None of it mattered, nothing mattered here in Cottonwood Springs now with Tom and Phil Morehead dead. Then Pres noticed a familiar little white building with a sign: *Paul Winthrop, M.D.* A lamp had been lit inside against the growing dusk. On an impulse Pres turned in. His impulse crystallized when a short, active man with a gray mustache came out of the inner room to greet him.

Doc Winthrop was older, but his cheeks were still red-veined and cheery, his eyes twinkling, his manner courteous as he said: "Something I can do for you?"

Pres smiled thinly. "I'm Pres Morehead, Doc."

The doctor put his whiskey glass down on the back room desk and shook his head in amazement. "Never would have known you, Pres. You've changed. Not only your face. Something inside has changed, boy. You don't look like . . . Cottonwood Springs."

Pres gave him a wry grin. "Maybe I helled around too much

before I drifted down to the Argentine and hooked up with a partner."

"Do all right?" Doc Winthrop had found another glass. He poured whiskey into it and handed it to Pres.

"We made out fair."

"Your father never said."

"He never knew," said Pres. "We didn't know ourselves whether we'd be bigger the next year or broke. My last two letters home weren't answered, so I thought I'd come back before they forgot all about me."

"Married, Pres?"

"No."

Doc Winthrop hesitated. "Better go back and enjoy life, boy. There's nothing around here for you any more."

Pres drained his whiskey glass and asked the question that was hanging between them. "Who killed my father and brother?"

Doc Winthrop sighed. "How do I know, Pres? You father never knew why your brother was shot. Phil had been a little wild, had been hanging around some wrong 'uns over at Corkscrew Flat. It looked like Phil feuded with someone who put a bullet in his back that night. Your father gave up then, Pres. Sold out to this brother and sister from California. He aimed to go to the Argentine and be near you. I guess he didn't tell anyone but me. The sheriff never got any good sign on his killer. Your father being the last Morehead around here, it's kind of drifted along. There's been rustling going on, and one thing and another to keep the sheriff busy."

"What might one thing and another be?"

"Sheriffs have been drifting in here hunting the Sugar Kid and his bunch, Pres. It kind of looks like they've holed up in the mountains through here somewhere, but they haven't been smoked out."

"Who might the Sugar Kid be?"

"A sweet name for a poison package," said Doc Winthrop. "Oregon, Idaho, and Montana were his stamping grounds. Things got too hot, and he pulled out with every sheriff for five hundred miles itching to get him. His bunch was almost cornered over in the San Juan River country. They fought it out and vanished."

"Any reason for thinking they're around here?"

"A Montana sheriff went over to Corkscrew Flat to look around and never came back," said Doc Winthrop. "Paddy O'Leary, kingpin over at Corkscrew Flat, says the Montana man didn't get there."

"O'Leary's word carry weight?"

"His guns do," said the little doctor. "Our sheriff hasn't spread it around, Pres, except to me, but Paddy O'Leary's been buying a heap of gumdrops lately. Corkscrew Flat never was partial to gumdrops before. Those northern sheriffs all brought the same story. Find a gunman with a pocketful of gumdrops and chances are you've got the Sugar Kid. Not much sense to it but they do say every man's got a weak spot. I'm betting gumdrops'll hang the Sugar Kid yet." The doctor reached for the whiskey bottle. "Take my advice, Pres. Go on back to the Argentine. You can't do any good around here. You might get into trouble if word gets out you're Pres Morehead."

"Gumdrops," mused Pres. "Funny . . . damned funny, ain't it? Who are those people who bought the Bar Z?"

"Two stubborn young fools who haven't got sense enough to run for their lives," said Doc Winthrop wryly. "Any day I'm looking for one or both of them to be hauled in on a wagon bed . . . or worse. The girl is too pretty for her own good, out there away from town on the Bar Z, and too near Corkscrew Flat."

"Tell me about them, Doc. Or do you know?"

"Better than other people around here," said Doc Winthrop. "I'm doctoring Bob Brady. They talk to me."

"Folks always did." Pres nodded.

"Kathleen Brady and Bob Brady grew up on a ranch and went to the cities. San Francisco, mostly, I take it, and Bob Brady studied some in Europe. He's an artist. The doctors told him he'd better get out of the city. He and his sister had enough money to buy the Bar Z from your father. They paid twelve thousand cash and took over the mortgage your father owed the bank."

"I didn't know the Bar Z was mortgaged."

"We had bad years, Pres. Anyway, your father took the cash from the bank, mostly big bills and a little gold, put it in a money belt, I guess, ready to leave for the Argentine. A few days later he rode out to the ranch to see the Bradys. They say he got there and left. It was about a week before he was found in the bottom of Bearhead Cañon, near his horse. The horse had been shot. Tom fell with him."

"And the money?"

"Gone," said Doc Winthrop reluctantly. "I hate to say this, Pres, but maybe you've already heard it. There hadn't been any rains. Old Injun Steve, who can track a shadow, showed where your father had ridden up the Bearhead Cañon Trail to the ranch . . . and then where he came riding back to where his horse was shot. And then another horse had come down the trail, over those tracks, and gone to the body, and then climbed back up the trail again. Injun Steve followed the tracks down to Turquoise Creek and lost 'em where cattle had been driven over the road. The sheriff did what he could, but there wasn't any proof he could pin for certain. Bob and Kathleen Brady took it pretty hard, and . . . well, you know how folks can get to talking about strangers."

Pres said nothing.

Doc Winthrop paused, and then continued slowly. "The Bradys had made a good buy from your father. There wasn't any trouble between them. And the Bradys aren't the kind who'd kill a man in cold blood for his money. But the dust from all that was still in the air when rustling trouble hit the Bar Z. Bob Brady wounded a rustler. Since then Bob Brady has been shot at. And instead of getting some sense and pulling out, those two have put up no trespassing signs, hired gun-packing hands, and put out word they'll run the Bar Z until hell freezes over, and all strangers are warned to keep outside their wire and stay healthy." Doc Winthrop sighed wearily. "Folks still had their back fur up over your father's death. They took the gun-hands as proof that the Bradys were tough and looking for trouble. There hasn't been much sympathy for them. And if you ask me how it's going to end," added Doc Winthrop with a worried frown, "I don't know. But my idea is that Bob and Kathleen Brady have got a grizzly by the tail and they're going to get clawed before it's over."

"Are the Bradys friendly with anyone at Corkscrew Flat?" Pres asked slowly.

"Hell, no," said Doc Winthrop. "They're hiring gunhands to keep out the rustlers. That ought to answer that."

"I rode out to the Bar Z today," said Pres. "I got shot at by a gunhand and told by the Brady girl I wasn't wanted around there."

"Can't understand that," Doc Winthrop said. "They'd be friendly to you."

"She didn't know who I was."

"That's why."

"Matter of fact," said Pres, "no one but you, Doc, knows I'm back. I registered at the hotel as John Emory."

"Any reason for that, Pres?"

"Not at the time. Just an idea." Pres stood up. "But I'll stay John Emory for a time, Doc."

Doc Winthrop's eyes did not always twinkle. Now the little

doctor was almost sober, almost stern as he got out of his chair. "You're not fooling me, Pres. You're looking for trouble now."

"I'm not trying to fool you, Doc. I'm just telling you not to say I'm back."

"Telling me?"

"Asking you."

The little doctor sighed and shook his head. "A doctor learns to keep his mouth shut, Pres. Sometimes the things he has to hold in are hard and hurtful. Many a time he has to wonder if he's done right. I'll be hoping you keep out of trouble."

III

Night had clamped down by the time Pres Morehead bought a .30-30 repeating rifle, three boxes of shells for the rifle, and two extra boxes of .45 shells for the old bone-handled side gun that had come out of his suitcase in the hotel room. On the way out of the hotel he had stopped in the dining room to wolf a quick meal. Now in the hardware store he added a saddle scabbard and a pair of blankets to his purchases.

Outwardly he was calm; inwardly grief scorched like blazing fire. Thought of Tom Morehead's drop to the bottom of Bearhead Cañon fanned the flame. A few hours before Pres had felt the cold, sinking feeling of helplessness as his horse scrambled uncertainly on the edge of the drop. Old Tom must have felt the same hollow feeling under the belt as his bushwacked horse launched into space, down, down to the water-smoothed rocks far below. Phil Morehead's death was different in some way. Maybe he had earned a little of it. You couldn't tell what feuding Phil had touched off at Corkscrew Flat. He had always been headstrong, high-tempered. But Tom Morehead hadn't deserved cold-blooded murder for the stake it had taken him a lifetime of hard work to earn. Doc Winthrop was a level-headed man you could listen to—kindly, too kindly for his own good sometimes.

Too quick to back up people he liked. You could bet Doc Winthrop hadn't seen the Brady girl eating gumdrops.

The livery stable had been left in charge of a lean, red-necked hostler who kept up a running fire of talk as he helped saddle a fresh horse for Pres. "You must be fixin' to travel with them blankets. I hear someone took a shot at you today. That scabbard and rifle looks like you're aimin' to burn back a little if it happens again."

"I hear rustlers are riding in these parts," said Pres shortly. "I'll feel better with a rifle."

Inwardly Pres damned himself for talking about the Bar Z gunman when he came in. The story would be going around town now. News of the rifle and the side gun would quickly be public property. Strangers would be wondering about the man called John Emory who had tangled with the Bar Z and ridden out of town armed. But he hadn't known about Tom Morehead until it was too late to avoid the talk—and gossip about John Emory would be nothing compared to the talk if it became known that Pres Morehead was back, riding the night trails heavily armed.

Corkscrew Flat was the halfway point. Once there had been mining activity in the rocky heights behind the flat and along the placer washings of Corkscrew Creek and the side cañons that slashed back and up into the mountains. Then Corkscrew Flat had been a rip-roaring center for the district. But the placers had worked out. Cattle and sheep outfits had pushed up to the mountains, grazing high on the succulent summer grasses. Corkscrew Flat had little left but whiskey, gambling, and dancing. You went to Corkscrew Flat when towns like Cottonwood Springs were too tame or too far away.

Now, tonight, under a thin moon Corkscrew Flat hadn't changed. The same ramshackle old plank buildings and cabins clustered at the upper end of the flat. Half a dozen separate little rivulets still brawled across the boulders and gravel. Willow brush along the water was thicker, if anything. Lights burned in some of the cabins. The Corkscrew Bar was lit. It hadn't been dark any night since it opened, Pres guessed.

The old trading store and bar had been built side-by-side, connected through the partition. The saloon had a dance floor, rooms at the back for gambling, a bar where forty men could line up. Tonight a generous dozen horses and several burros were at the hitch rack. Twice that many men were inside, Pres noted as he entered, cowmen, prospectors, miners, a few whiskey soaks. It was any man's guess where the rest were from—out of the gulches and mountain valleys, the grazing lands lower down, a little town or two this side of the mountains. But they were at Corkscrew Flat to drink and dance and gamble. The noise of it beat out into the night. Half a dozen girls had dancing partners, and one of the men whooped drunkenly above the music as Pres entered.

Eyes settled on him in quick, wary scrutiny. Strangers did well to walk softly here until they'd proved themselves. That Montana sheriff hadn't been the only man to disappear around Corkscrew Flat. A Mexican was playing a guitar and a giant Negro sawing on a fiddle. A pallid bartender with skin stretched like paper over his face bones set out whiskey and made change from an open cigar box on the backbar.

"Ain't seen you before," he remarked.

"I'm looking for Paddy O'Leary," Pres said.

"Paddy!" the bartender called.

Pres sensed he was being watched by the other men nearby. They watched furtively as O'Leary came leisurely from the end of the long bar. The man was short, fat, with a big pinkish face running up to the smooth expanse of a broad bald skull. He lacked even eyebrows. He might have been an overgrown baby, bland and cheerful. The two guns in open holsters under his arms seemed incongruous. Then, suddenly, Pres noticed that the pink face merely lacked expression. Even the pale blue eyes looked vacant as they ran over Pres. "I'm Paddy O'Leary, mister." The voice was soft, high-pitched, like a woman's voice.

"I'm looking up some old mine locations," Pres said. "They tell me in Cottonwood Springs you know these parts well."

The pale eyes considered him, then Paddy O'Leary smiled until his eyes seemed to sink in crinkles of fat and humor. "If I don't know, I can find out. You hunting old mines with a rifle, stranger?"

"Never can tell what you'll be hunting with a rifle." Pres smiled.

O'Leary seemed to think that hugely funny. "That's something to think over. Come back in my office. I'll do what I can for you."

The office was at the back, off a passage from which other doors opened. Poker chips rattled on a table behind one of the doors. An old roll-top desk and half a dozen wooden chairs furnished the office. A wall lamp threw yellow light over old calendars, pictures, Reward notices, tacked one on top of another on the walls.

O'Leary waved his visitor to a chair. Pres waited a moment and said bluntly: "No use beating around the bush, O'Leary. What will you do for five thousand dollars?"

O'Leary blinked. The old wired desk chair creaked as he dropped into it. "Cash?" O'Leary questioned.

Pres nodded.

Eyelids closed slowly down over the pale-blue eyes. When the eyes opened again, O'Leary asked: "Got the five thousand dollars on you, mister?"

"When I bring five thousand dollars to Corkscrew Flat, it'll be earned first," Pres said deliberately.

A shadow of disappointment passed over the pink face. Looking at Paddy O'Leary, Pres could understand why he was kingpin of Corkscrew Flat. His blank bulk seemed to spread an uneasy threat over the dingy little office. "Five thousand cash will buy a heap of anything, stranger. What mine were you thinking of?"

"Call it the O'Leary mine," said Pres coolly. "Maybe it's never paid dividends because it's never been worked right. I'm wondering if five thousand will bring pay ore out of it."

O'Leary's high chuckle shook his fat body. "That's a smart way to mine. What kind of ore are you looking for?"

"Who bushwacked Tom Morehead?" Pres asked.

The wired chair creaked, and Paddy O'Leary leaned forward, blank-faced, staring. "Who are you?" he asked abruptly.

"Not a lawman," said Pres.

"No," O'Leary agreed. "The law ain't putting up five thousand to find out about Morehead." The fat cheeks screwed up as he squinted. "Five thousand is easy to talk."

"I'll show it to you in the Cottonwood Springs bank tomorrow if you can deliver."

"Only someone close to the Moreheads would throw away five thousand like that." O'Leary's eyes closed. His voice dropped until he seemed to be speaking to himself. "I heard there was a son who went away years ago. . . ." The pale eyes snapped open, staring at Pres.

Pres stared back. "John Emory is the name. You'll find it on the Cottonwood Springs hotel register."

A big, soft hand lifted off the chair arm in a slight gesture. "Never mind the hotel register. I'm wondering why you rode out here to Corkscrew Flat to see me."

"I had an idea you might save me a heap of trouble. It would be worth five thousand."

"Set a thief to catch a thief?" asked O'Leary.

"If you want it that way."

The fat man's chuckle shook him again. "I like to do business with an honest man. No misunderstanding that way. You always know where you stand. An honest man with five thousand to spend. . . ."

"Well?" said Pres after a moment. Inside, he was like a stretched fence wire. He'd gambled heavily in tipping his hand on Corkscrew Flat like this. O'Leary might be tarred with some of the guilt himself. Another dead Morehead to end the matter might be worth more than $5,000 to O'Leary. You could bet that if Pres Morehead had guessed wrong, hell would be popping before long. But if he'd guessed right, he would have knowledge the sheriff couldn't get, knowledge he himself might not be able to trace down in years. Cheap at the price—cheap at any price when he thought of Tom Morehead taking that long fall to the cañon rocks.

O'Leary nodded, squinting again. "Interesting. I'd have to know . . ." The rattling doorknob brought O'Leary's bulk out of the chair with a quickness that was revealing. The big man could move with amazing lightness. "What is it?" his high-pitched voice cracked out sharply.

The bartender answered through the door. "Feller to see you, Paddy."

"Tell him to wait!"

"Says he's in a hurry. Got someone outside to see you."

"Coming," said Paddy O'Leary. He stood for a moment, considering. He caught a coat off a nail and shrugged into the sleeves, moving his arms to make certain the holstered guns were free and easy to get at. His pale eyes wandered about the room. "I'll be back," he said, and walked lightly out and closed the door.

Pres stared at the door a moment and drew the gun from his holster to make sure it was ready for use. Then he checked the rifle. He'd felt this way before, with his nerves crackling tension.

You couldn't read O'Leary, couldn't tell what he was thinking, what he was going to do. But you could be sure the man was dangerous, tricky, cold-blooded, calculating, ready to kill if it suited his purpose.

Pres stepped into the passage—and as quickly stepped back into the doorway, pulses hammering. He'd been able to see across the dance floor to the front half of the bar where O'Leary was meeting a man, turning to the front door. One look at the crossed cartridge belts, the leather chaps, the weather-beaten hat had been enough. A side view of the face had been final proof. McAlister, the man had been called by Kathleen Brady, McAlister, the hard young gunman riding for the Bar Z.

A harsh voice rose in the gambling game across the passage. "I'll raise you twenty! Gonna string along?"

Couples were dancing again. The wild rhythm in the Negro's fiddle sawed at Pres's nerves as he thought of the gumdrop the Brady girl had eaten. And now one of her gunmen had shown up on furtive business with Paddy O'Leary of Corkscrew Flat. There would be a door somewhere at the back of the building, Pres knew. He went back along the passage and was outside in the night a moment later, listening hard as he strained his eyes to the dark. The loom of the building took shape beside him, then one of the nearby cabins, the shadows of the brush clumps scattered across the flat. Moving carefully, Pres stepped around the corner of the building and edged toward the front. Somewhere ahead in the night O'Leary would be talking to the Bar Z gunman. And what O'Leary might be saying might mean a bullet in the back for Pres Morehead.

The window shade of O'Leary's office had a half inch of space at the bottom one could look through. Pres made sure the office was still empty, the door closed. The night seemed empty ahead. O'Leary might be returning to the office. If he found his visitor gone, any man's guess was good as to what might happen.

The wailing fiddle, the throbbing guitar, fell silent outside. Now the night noises were more audible. A horse stamped at the hitch rack in front. The water brawled softly in the little streams that threaded the rocky flat. Then a horse moved on the rocks off to the right. A moment later the impatient lift of a woman's voice came through the night quiet.

"You didn't say that before, O'Leary!" O'Leary's reply was too low to be understood, but Pres knew who had spoken. That cool, clear voice belonged to Kathleen Brady. She was angry. Her voice lifted again. "How much more money do you think you'll get?"

They were behind the nearest clump of willows—O'Leary of Corkscrew Flat and the Brady girl who Doc Winthrop had worried about because she lived nearer the flat than Cottonwood Springs. Thick as thieves, the two of them tangled in the same business, tarred with the same stick. Pres went over the rocky gravel toward the willows. He'd heard enough to damn the Bradys. He had to hear more now. Money wouldn't buy the truth of this from Paddy O'Leary.

Behind Pres a stone turned against another stone. He swung around, too late to escape the sharp order: "Stand still, you skunk!"

Pres was already pulling his gun. He'd taken a chance and lost. Caught now, he'd get short shrift. A gun licked red at him, blasting against the night quiet—two shots while he fired once. Then the top of his head seemed to explode, and he plunged down on the water-worn stones.

A kind of consciousness lingered. Pres could just about make out Paddy O'Leary shrilling furiously: "Get the hell back in there! Drinks on the house! This is a little private business that don't need attention!" Steps ran to the spot. O'Leary's high voice sounded again: "Is he dead?" A foot kicked Pres, and a rough hand closed tightly on his wrist. Then a match flared. "Hell, no. Only creased him. Who is he?" And that was the Brady gunman speaking. O'Leary swore angrily. "Don't know him. He walked in saying he wanted to ask some questions about old mines around here. I didn't have a chance to hear what he wanted to know. Did that Brady girl leave?"

A fog was closing down. Pres tried to fight it back. From a vast distance the young gunman snarled: "What do you think she did, with a gunfight under her nose? You ain't lying to me, O'Leary?"

"Why should I lie to you?"

"This fellow eased on the Bar Z today over that old cañon trail. I headed him off, and he claimed he was looking for the Morehead men. Now he turns up asking about old mines. Somebody's lying. What's he . . . ?"

Then pain-filled fog blotted out their voices.

IV

The next thing Pres heard was a man moaning, groaning, whimpering. The sound pushed the fog back, and he opened his eyes. A faint, flickering light threw wavering shadows on a low ceiling. Pres stirred and found himself in a bunk. There was something familiar about it, too. He had a quick, groggy feeling that he'd lain in this bunk before, looked at the same ceiling, the same rusty, old stovepipe over there in the corner, the same big nails driven into the logs by the door, and that big split log butting into the left side of the window, chinked in the split with mud.

The shock of remembrance wiped his mind clear, brought back the past with a rush. This was the old Bar Z line cabin up the shoulder of Grizzly Mountain. The cabin Tom Morehead had built for his winter riders who watched this end of the ranch for blizzard-trapped cattle. Many times young Pres Morehead had stretched in this bunk. Every detail of the room was etched on his mind. The moaning, the whimpering, had not stopped. Pres turned his head and saw no one. Trying to sit up was an effort. He almost groaned at the pain hammering under his scalp.

A candle end on the old sheet-iron stove gave off a flickering light. And on the dirt floor a man was lying, a fat, bald-headed man who stirred with restless pain, who weakly clawed his fingertips into the dirt, who groaned and whimpered. Paddy O'Leary's coat was gone. His guns were gone. His shirt hung in tatters. And the big man had been beaten, mauled, manhandled until he hardly looked human above the chest. Life still flickered in him, but the man had been broken cold bloodedly and cruelly.

Pres swung his legs down and sat up. The room swam dizzily. As he tried to control his whirling senses, the door opened on creaking hinges. The lanky young man who entered wore a six-gun and carried a rifle. He was thin-lipped, weak-chinned, and his careless swagger was half sneering.

"Decided to look around, huh?"

Paddy O'Leary cringed from the voice, moaning as he tried to inch back over the floor. Pres felt sick at the sight. No man deserved to be tortured into a wreck like that. "Who did it?" Pres jerked out.

"Good job, ain't it? He won't strut so big on Corkscrew Flat after this, the dirty snake. Take a good look at him. How d'you like it?"

"Want to know what I think about it?" asked Pres grimly.

"I asked you."

"Gut-shooting's too good for the men who did it."

The man was still grinning as he spat tobacco juice against the cold stove. "He's lucky. We might have built a fire and roasted him a little. Don't take any time to build a fire. Got sticks ready outside the door."

"What was the idea?"

"Caught him lying. He was seen cooking up something in his office with you. We brought him over here to think it over. Take another look at him."

"What was he cooking up?"

A wolfish grin preceded the answer. "We'll let you tell it. What O'Leary got ain't but a caution to what you'll get if you don't come clean on what you're up to around here. Look at him good if you think you're tougher than he is."

Pres stared at O'Leary. So they hadn't broken the man. They'd wrecked the thick body, but they hadn't broken O'Leary's spirit. He had evidently kept his mouth locked.

"How about it, Emory? Feel like talking?"

Pres moistened his lips. O'Leary hadn't told them that a Morehead had come offering $5,000 for information. And he wondered why O'Leary hadn't told and saved himself. "Did the Bradys order this?" Pres questioned harshly.

"Curious about the Bradys, ain't you?"

"That," said Pres, nodding at the floor, "would make anybody curious."

"Now ain't that nice?" The lanky young man grinned. "You're on Brady land, Emory. I'm on the Brady payroll. You was caught sneaking up on the Brady girl at Corkscrew Flat tonight. Figure it out, if it'll do you any good."

Pres stared at the man and turned his head to O'Leary, whimpering there on the floor. He thought of the Brady girl nibbling candy while she callously told of Tom Morehead's death and fury burned out the weakness in his body. The beat and hammer of the anger throbbed in the bullet furrow across his scalp. Doc Winthrop had been blind. Little Doc Winthrop— the one man who might have gotten at the truth by being shrewdly close to the Bradys—had been fooled by cool talk, by a woman's face. Tonight Doc had been back there in Cottonwood Springs, worrying about Kathleen Brady's safety, while she had ridden furtively over to deal with O'Leary, while her men were callously doing *this* to O'Leary. There had to be a reason for it. The answer seemed plain enough. The Bradys were afraid. A stranger asking for the Morehead men had made them wary. The same man caught talking with Paddy O'Leary had made them afraid. You had to be afraid of something to do this to a man. And they still must be afraid, for the stranger they still knew as John Emory was being threatened with the same treatment they had just given Paddy O'Leary.

"You've got your chance to talk now, Emory," the lanky young man drawled. "What about it?"

"What do you want to know?" Pres muttered.

"You ain't deaf. I asked what you're after around here. What was you after from O'Leary?"

"Mines," said Pres. "Old mines."

The wolfish smile broke out on the young man's face again. He drew his six-gun lazily. "That all you aim to say?"

From the edge of the bunk Pres gritted: "What would you like to hear?"

"The truth, damn you."

"What," asked Pres, "would sound like the truth?"

He was watching that fading, wolfish smile, watching for the gun, the hand that held it, trying to think of something in the cabin that could be used against the gun.

Tight-lipped, threatening, the man grated: "You're a lawman, ain't you?"

"No," Pres denied, watching the gun. He wasn't afraid of a killing shot if he didn't answer right. Not at first. Maybe a shot to wound him, to lame him, make him helpless, but he wouldn't be killed until there was nothing more to be gotten from him. Paddy O'Leary was proof of that.

"Damn it, you *are* a lawman! I'm gonna make you admit it!

Wolfing around on the Bar Z like you did and then sneaking to Corkscrew Flat. You're a damned lawman and you got a hold on O'Leary!"

"What kind of a hold?" Pres countered.

The weak-chinned face was tightening with anger. "Don't sit there firing questions at me! Are you gonna admit it?"

The candle was burning low. Little gusts of wind through the door made it flicker badly. The dark shadows danced and crawled on the walls, but there was enough light to shoot a man, torture a man. There was enough light for Pres to see the slow, convulsive movements of Paddy O'Leary at the back of the room. The Brady man moved a step nearer the bunk. His back was to the stove, to Paddy O'Leary. He lifted the gun muzzle suggestively like a club. Lips drew back over his teeth in the beginning of a snarl.

"How about it, feller?"

Paddy O'Leary had stopped whimpering, had lifted his head slightly. That mashed, gory caricature of a head that hardly seemed human was coming up out of the black shadows that clung to the floor. Pres dropped his eyes lest the truth be mirrored in them by a flicker of attention. He had to keep the other's attention on himself.

"Looks like you aim to have your own way," he said dully. "You've got me cold."

"So you *are* a lawman?"

Behind the lanky young man two eyes opened in the gruesome head. The bulk of Paddy O'Leary pushed up on his hands, up to the length of his arms. Only the heart of the man, deep in that wrecked body, could know what the effort cost. O'Leary's big arms were tense, trembling, shaking with the effort. He quaked and swayed with weakness, so that Pres felt the strain of it drawing him, tight and breathless, as he stared at the floor.

"I'll tell you what I came here for," muttered Pres heavily. "If it's got anything to do with the Bradys, I can't see it. I'm expecting to walk out of here on my way afterward. How about it?"

"Sure," agreed the other with a tight grin. "All I want's the truth. If it ain't got anything to do with the Bradys, you're in the clear. We'll forget all about it."

Paddy O'Leary got to his knees with another terrible effort. His great, puffy, gory lips made a convulsive movement that might have been a grin. O'Leary turned on his knees, without a sound. His shaking arm reached out toward the stove, to the flickering candle end. His big hand slapped down on the flame—and the cabin was plunged into instant blackness.

The gunman whirled toward the stove as the light went out, and Pres launched himself from the bunk, reaching for the other man's gun arm. The lanky young man cursed loudly as Pres crashed against him and caught his wrist. He tried to jerk free. They struck the stove and knocked it over. The stovepipe tumbled over their heads. A savage twist turned the gun toward Pres. Two crashing shots spat red fire close to his face, deafened him. The bullets just missed his arm and shoulder. Pres got his other hand back of the gun and swung the muzzle away.

Out of the darkness, a hand clawed against his face, found his eyes, tried to gouge out an eye. The sharp agony in Pres's eye socket was like fire burning into the brain. Sick with helplessness, he caught at the hand and hurled the other man away as, with a twisting wrench, he jerked the gun free from his grip. The jump, the twist to one side, saved Pres from the roaring shot that sought him in the blackness.

He tripped over a piece of the stovepipe, rolled across the floor as two more shots crashed out of the corner. Then he found himself up against the wall opposite the bunk. The shots had missed him—and as he came up to a knee, the quiet of death shut down inside the cabin. Five shots had been fired, he figured. The six-gun might hold another, or it might be empty if the gunman had been carrying an empty shell.

Seconds passed while Pres hugged the wall and his shot-deafened ears returned to normal. He heard a faint, metallic click. Then a handful of empty shells scattered over the floor near the door. The thin, gritting voice of the lanky young man knifed from the corner. "Now, damn you! I'll get you now!" A piece of stovepipe clattered softly as a foot struck it. The gunman swore softly.

Crouched there against the wall, Pres desperately balanced the odds. He might dive through the door before a bullet cut him down, but that would leave Paddy O'Leary with the Brady killer. Pres slid his hand along the floor. Somewhere nearby was the rifle the gunman had dropped. Pres touched an old packing box that had been used for a seat. It came up soundlessly in his straining grip. He threw the box and rolled across the floor as it struck.

The gunman yelled, the box smashed down on the stove, and the gun blasted lead through the darkness again. A cold shock went through Pres's leg as a bullet found him. And his groping hand found the wooden stock of the rifle.

The gunman was shouting furiously. Low down in the corner, the gun blasted again and again as Pres came up to his feet with the rifle. The Brady man was floundering against the stove. He fired again as Pres jumped to the spot, clubbing the rifle by the barrel. The gunstock struck a body, struck it again, and the Brady gunman cried out. Pres clubbed savagely at the sound. He felt the wooden stock smash against a yielding object. A foot struck his leg, quivered, and lay still.

Pres dropped to his knees, groping. He felt the overturned stove, and his hand came against the motionless figure beside it. They'd left matches in his pocket. He scratched a match against the stove, and the scene leaped at him. The Brady man sprawled there with his jaw battered out of shape, blood crawling over soot-blackened skin. He still gripped the six-gun. Paddy O'Leary lay there, too, one arm stretched out above his head, and the big hand still clamped in a vise-like grip about the Brady man's ankle.

Everything was suddenly as plain as if the cabin had been lit, and Pres had witnessed the moves. Paddy O'Leary had fallen back to the floor with the candle stub in his hand. The candle lay there beside him. But down in that mashed, mauled head, Paddy O'Leary had been thinking while the gun crashed and the fight raged in the dark. Paddy O'Leary had known what was happening, had known when the Brady gunman reloaded that Pres Morehead faced odds too great for any man. In the darkness O'Leary had reached out and gripped the gunman's ankle. Grimly, desperately O'Leary had held that ankle while lead smashed into his already-mauled body. Dying, Paddy O'Leary had held on grimly to give Pres Morehead his chance.

Bullet holes were there in O'Leary's half-naked torso—one just above the belt, the other high up on the chest. Little round reddish holes from which the blood was reluctant to come. They hardly looked dangerous. Pres caught up the candle, lit it with the dying match, and held it in his left hand and felt for O'Leary's heart. The faint flutter and beat of that heart was almost impossible to feel, but Paddy O'Leary felt something, sensed something. A quiver of life ran through O'Leary. He stirred.

Pres tried to loosen the fingers clamping on the gunman's ankle. He could not pry them free. "It's all right, O'Leary," he said. "All right now. Let's go."

O'Leary stirred again. The monstrous puffed lips, bloody, frothy now, moved in what might have been a smile. He released the ankle, and his eyes opened and stared at the candle. He lay motionlessly, as if dead, but the bloody froth on his lips bubbled slightly.

"Can you understand me, O'Leary?"

The fat man moved his head, and then began to choke, gasp. After long moments the blood cleared from his throat, and he lay with his mouth open, gasping. He was in a pool of blood, dying fast. Pres spoke clearly. He had to make the man understand.

"He's done for, O'Leary. You did it. But he shot you. There's nothing I can do for you. Understand?"

O'Leary's head barely moved, but it was a nod, clearly a nod.

"You never told me who killed Tom Morehead," Pres said. "This is your chance, O'Leary. If there's anyone you want the five thousand to go to, I'll see that it's paid."

The warped smile on the puffed, battered lips was plain now. So was the slight shake of O'Leary's head.

"No one you want the money paid to?"

Again the negative.

Hot candle grease slid down Pres's fingers as he bent lower. "Tell me, O'Leary. I'm going after the men who did this to you. I've got a hunch it'll be the same outfit that killed my father. Listen, the Sugar Kid is mixed in it, isn't he?"

Now blood swelled up in O'Leary's throat as the man strangled and gasped again. When the spasm passed, O'Leary looked like a dead man, but his eyes were still open.

Pres tried again. "Is the Sugar Kid mixed up with the Bradys?"

O'Leary's head barely moved, but it was a nod.

"And they're the bunch who killed Tom Morehead?"

O'Leary nodded again. His mashed mouth tried to say something, but the words were only a mumble that broke off into another spasm of choking. This time the attack did not stop. On and on it went until blood was gushing from O'Leary's mouth. And suddenly the big man shivered and lay, limp and quiet. This time his eyes were closed. Now there was no heartbeat, no life left.

V

Shaking from the strain, Pres got to his feet with the candle. Now he knew. No court of law, no jury would hang a man on what he could tell. In life Paddy O'Leary might not have convinced a jury, but in dying he had convinced Pres Morehead. The Brady gunman's jaw was smashed. He might be unconscious all night. Pres buckled the man's gun belt around his waist, reloaded the six-gun. The rifle was useless.

On a sudden thought Pres kneeled down and searched the Brady man. He found a fat leather money belt next to the skin. The belt pockets held gold coins and bills—two $500 bills and several $100s. Pres looked at the money. His hand began to shake; his eyes grew moist. A ranch hand would not be carrying $500 bills. No cowhand, no gunman would have them when he could get smaller money. Only a man like Tom Morehead, drawing thousands from the bank to carry in a money belt, would get bills like this. Tom Morehead had been carrying this money—and it was his blood that stained the edges of the bills so darkly.

Pres shoved the money into his pocket, blew out the candle, and walked outside. The gunman's horse was tied to the silvery trunk of a small aspen.

Pres mounted and started the horse down the slope of Grizzly Mountain, on the trail he had often ridden as a boy, to Turquoise Creek and the Bar Z ranch house. His watch was gone, so he could not tell the time, but the thin moon had dropped far down on the sky. Long hours had passed since the guns had roared on Corkscrew Flat. But the night had still more hours, and another day lay ahead, and the savage anger that rode now with Pres Morehead would last until this business was finished. The money weighted down his pocket with bitter reminder. Blood was soaking the inside of his left riding boot. The wound was beginning to hurt. The bullet had scored deeply in the calf muscles of the leg.

The Brady gunman had smelled of liquor. Hidden in one of the saddle pockets Pres found a half-empty pint bottle of whiskey. He poured the liquor into the wound, then took a long gulp before he finished tying up the leg. He soaked the bandage with what was left of the whiskey. The drink brought some strength as he rode down through the thinning trees to the lower range. More Brady gunmen might be on his trail tonight, heading for the line cabin to see what had happened to Pres Morehead. But only the night wind in the pines, the hoofs of the horse, the creak of saddle leather, and the rustle of brush broke the night's quiet.

Down off Grizzly Mountain, through the foothills to the little bluffs along Turquoise Creek, Pres followed the familiar trail. Half a mile from the bluffs the horse threw up his head. The moon was gone, but there was enough starlight to see the pricked ears, the horse testing the wind. Pres reined up and tried to read the night. He thought he heard the faint, far-off call of a man, then the bawl of a cow. He rode on cautiously. After a time he was sure he heard cattle.

He reached the Turquoise Creek bluffs, a hundred feet high, with the creek shallows rippling along the bottom, and the ranch road following the other side in the long bend the creek made with the curve of the bluffs. Then he tied the horse a hundred yards back from the bluffs, went forward on foot, and looked down into the black drop with wary amazement.

Down there on the ranch road cattle were moving. Not a few cows and steers. Not a small bunch. A trail herd was strung out down there for a quarter of a mile by the sounds, cows, calves, and steers. The point men had long passed. The drags were moving abreast when Pres reached the bluffs. A match flared across the creek as a drag rider lit a cigarette. A moment later another match flared. Pres heard the faint sound of their voices as they exchanged comments.

Bar Z cattle were on the move, but not to pasture, not trail herding this way in the middle of the night. Uncertainly Pres stood there, trying to fathom the mystery. Brady cattle moving hurriedly, steadily toward the ranch boundaries. Doc Winthrop had spoken of rustlers working on the Bar Z and other ranches. Against that threat the Brady gunmen had been riding the Bar Z fences. Now where were the gunmen?

If the men down there were not rustlers, then the Bradys were sending their own beef off the Bar Z furtively, hurriedly in the night. That meant fear. And it would be fear of Paddy O'Leary and the man who called himself John Emory, fear of a lawman getting close to the Bar Z, to the Bradys, to the proof of Tom Morehead's murder, to the hiding place of the Sugar Kid and his killers. O'Leary's dying nod had said the Sugar Kid was on the Bar Z with the Bradys.

Pres walked back to the horse and followed the trail upstream to the end of the bluffs and down across the creek to the road. There he hesitated. The cattle had passed beyond hearing. The road was empty. If the Bradys were clearing the beef off the Bar Z, they'd be moving out of the ranch house, too—and the Cottonwood Springs bank would have land and fences and buildings and nothing else for its mortgage on the Bar Z. Pres pointed the horse toward the ranch house and the Bradys.

He met no one. Half a mile from the ranch house he swung off across the range, circling widely and coming through the scattered brush to the draw where the ranch buildings lay. Now dawn was not more than two hours off. The stars were bright; the air was sharply cool. Down there in the flat the bunkhouse was dark; the corrals seemed empty. Only a house window showed light.

Pres tied the horse at the edge of the draw and went down the slope on foot. He came up behind the corrals, and they were empty. So was the horse corral. The bunkhouse door was half open. No one snored or moved inside. Gun cocked, Pres stepped silently inside and struck a match. The flare showed him empty bunks, a careless litter on the floor as if men had gone through their war bags hastily and discarded everything not needed.

Tight-lipped, Pres moved to the friendly log-and-stone house that had been a part of his boyhood. The window was still lit. A saddled horse stood out in front. Behind that window lay the big main room, to the right of the center hall. A murmur of voices came from inside.

Clearly enough a man said: "Gimme that bottle again, as long as it's free."

And somebody else said: "Deal the cards, Pete, if we've got to sit here."

Pres did not need light to find the latch and ease the door open. His feet moved unerringly in the dark hall to the closed living room door. Thumbing back his gun hammer, he shoved the door open and stepped inside.

"Hoist 'em!" he bit out.

Hands flew up.

"Hell! Now what?"

A lamp burned dimly in a wall bracket at the end of the room. Five men had been playing poker at the center table. Pres scowled at their strained, questioning looks. Grizzled Ed Safford and Hi-Low Kenny sat there with unreadable faces. Fifteen years back they had been riding for Tom Morehead. The next two were younger men, cowhands—and the fifth was Doc Winthrop.

"Well, Doc," said Pres as he approached the table, "you fooled me."

Doc Winthrop looked unhappy. He was pale. His voice was thick and husky as he said: "Just take it easy now."

"Shut up," Pres said through his teeth. "I'll find out damned quick what you're doing here. Stand up!" Pres ordered the nearest young man. "Back to me! Got a money belt?"

"Nope," denied the young man uneasily.

Pres made a quick one-handed search, did the same thing to the other young cowhand. Neither man seemed to be carrying cash.

"Sit down," Pres told them. Bitterness made his voice shake. He took the paper money from his pocket and showed it to them. "I took this off one of your riders a while ago. It's all I needed to know. Where's that Brady girl and her brother?"

"We don't know where the Bradys are. Take it easy," Doc Winthrop urged.

"Your talk about the Bradys," Pres said bitterly, "maybe you didn't know this cut-throat outlaw called the Sugar Kid had been training with them. Maybe you didn't know the Brady girl made night rides over to Corkscrew Flat to see Paddy O'Leary. Maybe you don't know the Bar Z cattle are being moved off tonight. You've got a hell of a lot to explain."

Doc Winthrop looked like an old man now, and his voice was dry and weary when he spoke. "There's nothing I can do. I didn't know all that . . . and you haven't done any good telling it. Don't move. Look there in the kitchen door behind you."

"It's buckshot, brother! Don't move is right!"

The speaker had been sitting there beyond the dark doorway behind Pres, invisible unless you looked closely. Now he was on his feet, thick-chested, beefy, white teeth gleaming in a short black beard as he enjoyed the moment.

"Pitch that smoke iron down on the floor," he ordered.

"Don't try anything wild, Pres," Doc Winthrop begged. "He'll cut you in two with buckshot. Throw down that gun like he says."

The shotgun was cocked and ready. Silently Pres tossed his gun on the floor.

Grizzled Ed Safford sighed with audible relief. "Thought you was gonna get it sure," the old Bar Z man said.

Pres eyed the group bitterly. "I didn't think I'd catch you in anything like this, Safford."

"Me, neither," Safford retorted. "I ain't sure what it's all about, but do you figure I'd be setting in the living room playing cards at this time of night, if a gun wasn't keeping me at it? Or Doc, either? You just cold-jawed yourself in on a stew pot full of hell and made it worse."

The bearded man came leisurely into the room, cradling the shotgun. His finger cuddled the trigger, and he was grinning unpleasantly. "You've got a hell of a lot to explain," he said to Pres. "Where'd you get that black all over your face and hands?"

Pres noticed then that soot had smeared his hands and clothes, his face too, he reckoned. "Knocked over a stovepipe," he said briefly.

"Gimme that money." The bearded man looked at the bills, shoved them into his pocket. His smile turned ugly. "So Slim let you get away? He must be dead then. Serves him right for letting it happen. And you know all about the Sugar Kid and O'Leary and who kilt that old codger in Bearhead Cañon, and you're on the warpath to do something about it?"

Pres watched the man closely. The unpleasant grin grew broader.

"And you got a line on these men, too, and got it all figured out. All you need is the Bradys now and the Sugar Kid, and you'll be all set."

Pres stood silently. Some of this made sense, some didn't. But the buckshot gun made sense—and the bearded man was working up to something.

"The Bradys," he told Pres, "have lit out and won't be back. The Kid and the rest of the boys have gone with 'em. I'll be tailing along after I hold this bunch here for a day or so. But you're the skunk who caused all this upset. You come looking to raise hell, and I'm gonna give it to you with a load of buckshot."

He meant it. The glint of it was in his look, in the tense curl of his finger over the shotgun trigger.

"Going to butcher me without giving me a chance at a gun?" Pres asked slowly.

"That's right. Get down on your knees and beg if it'll make you feel better."

Ed Safford's sudden yell filled the room like thunder.

"Look at this!"

Ed's hand had already hurled a fistful of poker chips off the table. He was diving sideways off his chair behind the table as he yelled. And Pres, on a hair-trigger waiting for the shotgun to bellow death, jumped sideways as the bearded man looked toward the table and his head jerked as the poker chips struck his face.

The shotgun's roar shook the room as both barrels went off. Wadding and part of a shot charge tore the side of Pres's coat. The heavy recoil drove the bearded man back a step. He hurled the gun at Pres and jumped backward, swearing as he clawed for his holstered gun.

The empty shotgun half numbed Pres's arm as he knocked it aside in the air and dived for the man, but the six-gun was streaking out of the holster and the bearded man was leaping back out of reach. Then shots from the table behind Pres came deliberately and evenly spaced. Two bullets hit the bearded man in the chest, one centered on his face. His hands flew up helplessly as he sprawled back through the kitchen doorway and lay there.

Ed Safford got up from his crouching position behind the table and blew smoke from the muzzle of the gun Pres had tossed on the floor. "Didn't think I could make it," said Ed laconically. "But you was a goner anyway, Pres. I made the gamble."

Pres looked at his hand. It was unsteady. "I feel shaky that way," he admitted. "Some gamble, Ed. But how come? He might have got you, too."

Ed's reply was brusque. "Think we could 'a' sat there and watched Tom Morehead's boy get butchered like a barbecue beef? I seen Hi-Low inching a fist toward the whiskey bottle and knowed he was aiming to chuck it. And the doc was getting stiff in his chair like he was going over the top of the table. I jest happened to beat 'em to it."

"Just happened," said Pres. "Ed, *I'm* ashamed. Doc . . . Hi-Low, I'm apologizing."

One of the young cowhands, still pale and shaken, pleaded: "What'n hell is it all about?"

"You heard," said Pres.

Doc Winthrop nodded. "We heard, Pres, but we still don't know much. I got to worrying about you tonight and finally hitched up my buggy and drove out here to see the Bradys. Some gunmen met me down the road, took my team and buggy, and brought me to the bunkhouse, where these *hombres* were being held under guard. After a time we were brought into the house here and left with that man watching us. We were told we'd be held here a day or so, and anyone trying to get away would be shot."

"It was those damn' gunmen the Brady woman hired," Ed Safford grunted. "We'd turned in at the bunkhouse when this McAlister rode up and called a couple of 'em outside. Next thing the four of us had guns stuck in our faces and were told to be quiet and not ask any questions. Are the Bradys really skinning out, Pres?"

"I'll tell you what I know," said Pres, and did.

They listened silently, with hardening faces.

"I can understand some things now," Ed Safford said. "It was plain to us she hired those gunfighters herself. Her brother was kinda puny and didn't stir out much. She gave 'em orders . . . mostly through this young McAlister. Told us regular hands to go on with the work and the new men would look out for rustlers and help us when they were needed. We never did know where she hired 'em. They was a close-mouthed bunch. But we figured she must be on the right track. There wasn't any more rustling after they started riding the fences." Safford spat, shook his head. "And all the time she was thick with O'Leary over at the flat."

Hi-Low was a lean-jawed man with a slow way of talking. Now Hi-Low's voice had a hard, rasping edge. "I knowed there was talk about Tom Morehead's murder, but I couldn't figure the truth of it laid here with us. They figure on two, three days' clear start. Are they gonna get away with it?"

Doc Winthrop had been listening in troubled silence. "Men," he said heavily, "I'm only a country doctor, but I've brought folks into the world and closed their eyes on the way out. I've talked to folks when their hearts were breaking and when the fear of death was on them. I've heard their secrets, their sorrows, and their happinesses. None of you has ever had reason to think me a fool."

"Hell, no, Doc," agreed Hi-Low awkwardly. "Who said so?"

"Then don't call me a fool for saying Kathleen Brady and her brother aren't guilty of all this," said Doc Winthrop simply. "I sat by young Brady's bed while he told me of the things he meant to do after he got well here on the Bar Z. I heard the truth of it in his sister's voice when she walked outside with me and asked for me to hope that their ideas would work out. Tears were in her eyes. That girl never would have let a man be tortured as this man O'Leary was tortured. Pres, Hi-Low, Ed . . . go easy. Those two aren't guilty of all this."

An embarrassed silence followed. Pres broke it slowly. "Then who is guilty, Doc?"

"I don't know," Doc Winthrop confessed.

"They're gone," reminded Ed Safford.

"I know." Doc Winthrop nodded. "I'm just asking you to go slow in your judgments until you're sure."

"That oughtn't to be hard," Pres said. "We'll find the lot of them, and the truth will be there. How many of these gun artists did the Bradys hire?"

"Seven," said Ed Safford.

"Including the man I left up on the mountain and this one?"

"Uhn-huh."

"Which leaves five, unless they've picked up more. They're got their hands full of cattle and making time. They're not looking for trouble yet unless they sent a man to that line cabin and found me gone . . . which I don't think happened."

"Five," Ed Safford said grimly. "And five of us, leaving out Doc." Ed looked at the two younger hands. "Joe, Sam, you two ain't said much. How much fight you got left?"

Sam was a tanned, open-faced young man with a quick likable grin. "Plenty fight," he said. "But how about guns? They took ours."

"We've got a shotgun, two six-guns, and there's a rifle back there in the kitchen," Safford said. "Ought to be some more guns if we search the place good."

"The horse corral is empty," Pres said. "They took everything. My horse is tied on the rise behind the bunkhouse. There's another out front. And that's all."

"Joe," said Safford, "how about that bunch you ran out of the east flat today? Can you and Sam haze four, five back here

158

a-burning?"

"If they ain't too hard to find in the dark."

"Git going then. There ain't been time to clean out this ranch. They just were lucky we'd been working the cattle into the home pasture for a count and cut. Or maybe it wasn't luck," Ed growled. "Maybe it was planned. Sorry, Doc, I can't help thinking out loud."

"I don't blame you," Doc Winthrop said. "I'm just hoping the gun sights stay off Kathleen Brady and her brother until you know what you're doing. There was a gun hanging in the bedroom closet. It may still be there."

They had the ranch house and outbuildings to themselves in the search for guns, cartridges, extra saddles. Doc Winthrop noticed Pres limping and insisted on examining his leg. His doctor's kit had been taken with his buggy, but there was a medicine chest in the house. He cleaned and bandaged the leg and the furrowed scalp, and Pres took time to wash himself. A rifle, two gun belts, and several boxes of shells had been overlooked in the bunkhouse. More guns and cartridges were found stored away in the ranch house. Saddles and bridles had been left in the saddle shed.

"All we need," said Ed Safford, "is horses."

Ten minutes later drumming hoofs brought them outside with guns ready, then running to guide the rush of a full dozen horses into the waiting corral.

"Had luck and found 'em at this end of the flat near the water," Joe said.

" 'Bout time we had some luck!" Hi-Low answered, slamming the gate. "Somebody light that lantern while I hang a rope on one of these ornery broomtails."

Minutes later, when they were mounted, Pres said: "Doc, why not ride back to Cottonwood Springs and tell the sheriff?"

"Tell him the Bradys are moving their cattle off their land?"

"Tell him about O'Leary, and the money I found, and this outlaw the Bradys are running with."

Doc Winthrop's answer was heavy. "If a Cottonwood Springs posse thought it had proof the Bradys caused your father's death, Pres, the Bradys would be doomed right then. I'll not be the one to ride for the sheriff before I know the truth. I want to see the Bradys first."

"I guess we all do," said Pres. "Let's go."

VI

The cold faint light of the new day found them riding hard beyond Bar Z land into the foothill country that sloped to the northwest toward the Parrados River, two days' ride away. At a short halt to breathe the horses, Ed Safford scowled over the cigarette he was rolling.

"This don't make sense, Pres. They're leaving a trail a kid could foller. A couple of days this way and they'll be in the Parrados Valley, smack near the Parrados sheriff and other ranchers and the railroad."

"And the railroad shipping pens and cattle buyers," Pres said. "The Bradys have a legal right to drive their cattle to Parrados and sell every head for the best money they can get. For cash money that'll leave them free to travel."

"Cottonwood Springs would be nearer."

"And hostile to them. Questions would be asked. The bank might have something to say about it. In Parrados," he pointed out, "they can sell and leave quick. The Bradys warned the public off the Bar Z. Their gunmen got folks out of the habit of coming around. Cottonwood Springs folks don't get over on this side of the mountains much. A gunman stayed on the ranch to make sure you men didn't carry word away, and another stayed to find out from me what trouble they could expect.

They've got plenty of time to sell and travel before the word gets around."

"Chances are they'll grub and water and grass a little when they reach Porcupine Creek," Hi-Low guessed. "They won't want to gaunt the critters down too much. We'll ketch 'em down there in a couple of hours."

"And chances are," Pres added, "they'll be watching the back trail. We'd better cut off to the left and hit the creek lower down."

The rest agreed. They circled off into the higher foothills and rode down through the broken country toward Porcupine Creek. The sun was high and bright when they watered the horses and turned upstream beyond the creek.

"Scatter out, so one man just sights the next," Pres said. "I'll take the point nearest the creek and pull my hat off if I see anything. The rest of you do the same."

A mile farther on they had scattered until Ed Safford was the only man in sight, and Ed was hard to keep track of, riding well off to the left and behind. In this broken country one could not see far. And sound did not carry. Suddenly Pres topped a swell of land and looked down a slope onto a big grassy flat where a trail herd was grazing. He had not realized the Brady herd could be so near. There was a chuck wagon, a two-horse buggy, and two riders circling the cattle. The rest of the crew was afoot by the chuck-wagon fire, evidently eating. And keen eyes were watching, for the nearest rider yelled something toward the chuck wagon and pointed his horse toward the slope of the rise. A moment later another rider swung up on a horse by the wagon and came galloping.

Pres watched with narrowing eyes. His face was set, hard and bleak. The rider coming from the chuck wagon was a woman. It was the Brady girl, coming of her own free will to look the stranger over. Bitterness that had been building up against

Kathleen Brady and her gun crew held Pres motionless, watching her. He deliberately left his hat on as she approached. This was Pres Morehead's quarrel now, and only the Brady girl and one rider were coming.

Halfway up the slope the rider waited for her. They exchanged a few words, and the man came on ahead of her. He was grinning and near enough now for Pres to see that it was not McAlister but a younger man, double gunned, carrying a rifle in his saddle boot to match the rifle by Pres's leg. The Brady girl wore a buckskin riding skirt, short jacket, small sombrero. Even at a distance it seemed to Pres that the sleepless night had left her weary, tired, had dulled the fire that had blazed out from her spirit only yesterday.

"Howdy!" her man called.

"Howdy," Pres said curtly.

"Live around here?"

"Riding through."

"Alone?" the man asked as he rode up.

"More or less," said Pres. "I wasn't looking for a trail herd."

The man didn't know him. The night had left Pres Morehead an unshaven, soiled range rider, but the Brady girl would know him quickly enough. Pres sat loosely, watchfully, waiting for her recognition. Her man was speaking as she came to them.

"We're moving some beef to the railroad. The lady runs the Bar Z brand over against Grizzly Mountain. She says grub and coffee are hot down at the chuck wagon if you feel like a bite. Ain't that right, ma'am?"

She reached them in time to hear the last. Pres felt his nerves tightening to the explosive point as she looked at him stonily and nodded. "If you're hungry," she said.

"I'm not," said Pres.

Her white throat moved as she swallowed. She knew him. The hand she rested on the saddle horn trembled. Pres noted the men down at the chuck wagon, watching them. The Brady rider was eyeing him narrowly, and his smile had thinned.

"Ride down and talk with the boys, stranger. How about it . . . ma'am?"

"We'd . . . we'd like to have you," Kathleen Brady said.

Pres met her glance squarely for an instant. The fear that leaped at him was so poignant and startling that Pres sat there, shocked and puzzled. But from the corner of his eye he saw the young gunman touch a spur to his horse and move carelessly over to the right.

"Nice horse you've got," the man said.

Pres nodded, and saw the man trying to read the brand.

"That's a Bar Z horse, ain't it?"

Pres had been expecting the streaking draw that started now with no other warning. His own hand slapped to his gun butt and whipped up, triggering lead with equal suddenness. Amazement flashed on the Brady man's face as roaring lead knocked him sprawling from the saddle. His horse squealed and bolted like unleashed lightning. Kathleen Brady cried out as if her own flesh and blood had been shot. For an instant her words failed to make sense to Pres.

"You've killed him!" she cried. "You've killed Bob! Oh, why did it have to be this way?"

The gunman rolled over on the ground and lifted his gun. Pres spurred hard to get out of the way. It was hard to shoot a man sprawled out and dying. And the second Pres hesitated was too long. The gun crashed twice—and the horse under Pres stumbled down to his knees as Pres swept the rifle out of the boot and jumped. The Brady man was through. The gun had dropped from his limp hand, and his eyes were closed, but he was dying with a snarling smile of satisfaction on his young face. Grimly Pres ended his horse's suffering with a bullet and whirled on the Brady girl.

She sat there, pale and frozen, as Pres gritted at her: "That your brother?"

"That man?" Her voice broke. "My brother's down there with the rest of them! A prisoner! And they'll kill him now as they said they would!"

She had come without guns. There was no danger from her. Pres was looking toward the chuck wagon. Down there men were already spurring horses toward the trouble.

"Nobody's getting killed down there," Pres said coldly. "What are you trying to tell me?"

She was dismounting, dragging her horse to him. "Take this horse and ride," she begged huskily. "They'll kill you. Maybe I can make them believe you took my horse. They'll . . . they'll *have* to believe me."

"Aren't you the boss down there?" Pres bit out.

"Do I act like I'm the boss?" she cried. "Are you blind? They took over the ranch last night. They're driving our cattle off to sell. They're taking my brother and me along to sign the sale papers. We're helpless. I had to ride here and ask you down there so they could see who you were. They're holding my brother. They told me I'd better bring you back."

"Get on that horse and ride like hell!" Pres snapped at her. "I'll hold them."

"No . . . no! That isn't the way. I'll go back to the chuck wagon. It's the only chance I've got to help Bob. They need us both until the cattle are sold. Oh, please. Don't stand there making it harder."

Cattle were scattering before the gunmen spurring across the flat, four men—and they came with rifles out and their purpose plain. Two of them started to circle out to the right, and one swerved off to the left, and one came straight on. You could see they meant to surround the dismounted man and cut off his escape. Pres caught the dying man's six-gun off the ground and took the reins from Kathleen Brady.

"If I don't see you again," Pres said, "Doc Winthrop will tell you who I am. And if I don't see Doc again, tell him I was wrong and he was right." Pres swung onto her horse and grinned down at her. "I wish I had time to tell you myself," he said as he thumbed fresh cartridges into the guns.

He holstered one gun and kept the other in his hand. She cried out in protest as he put her horse into a gallop down the slope toward the chuck wagon and the gunmen coming for him. The man riding straight at him was the hard-faced young gunman called McAlister. Somehow Pres had expected that. He had been increasingly certain as to who McAlister must be. Paddy O'Leary would have known. Pres thought of O'Leary and Tom Morehead as he cocked his six-gun and spurred hard down the slope.

The other riders were swerving back, but they were too far away now. They would not be there when Pres Morehead met the Sugar Kid. Dust was rising above the milling herd as the outside cattle began to break away toward higher ground. McAlister reined to an abrupt stop and threw up his rifle. Pres heard the close scream of lead. Then a second bullet came still closer. Now he was within six-gun range, and, as he opened fire, McAlister slammed the rifle into the scabbard, drew both his handguns, and came on, firing with rapid precision. A fear-maddened steer bolting close made McAlister's horse shy. Pres shoved his emptied gun inside his belt and snatched out his other weapon.

A bullet clipped across his shoulder. Another smashed into his left arm. With guns roaring, they rushed together. The snarling grin on McAlister's face was plain. No fear there. A killer was working at his trade and taking his chances. Then one of McAlister's guns flew through the air as his arm went limp from a grazing bullet. Three shots left. Pres held them until the last moment—and fired them in a roaring burst that carried the memory of Paddy O'Leary and Tom Morehead. McAlister snatched desperately at the saddle horn. He was clawing at the air and falling, as his horse swerved aside and Pres flashed past.

Pres awkwardly tried to reload as he rode through the stampeding cattle to the chuck wagon and Doc Winthrop's buggy. He could barely use the wounded arm. Now through the dust haze and thunder of cattle hoofs, bullets were shrilling as the other three riders closed in, working their rifles. Clutching his rifle, Pres made a flying dismount at the chuck wagon.

One look was enough to place the thin, pale, young man struggling there on the ground with wrists and ankles that had been tied with pigging strings. Bob Brady bore a striking resemblance to his sister.

"Keep down!" Pres yelled.

Using the back of the chuck wagon for a rest, Pres sighted the rifle carefully on the nearest rider. The man was fairly in the sights when Pres squeezed the trigger. As he threw another shell into place, Pres saw the rider slide out of the saddle. Two gunmen were left—and they suddenly seemed to realize that the chuck wagon made a perfect fort for an expert rifleman. They swung sharply around in the dust haze and bent low as they rode for cover.

Pres sighted on one man, missed, tried again, and got the horse. The rider staggered up from the fall and broke into a limping run for the higher ground. Then he stopped as other riders burst over the rise and raced down the slope. Caught by surprise, the last rider whirled his horse toward the nearby brush along Porcupine Creek.

Pres stepped out from the chuck wagon and watched two horsemen race across the slope at an angle to cut off the man. The crackle of gunshots came faintly through the last of the stampede, and the outlaw's horse plunged into a rolling fall.

The rider got to his knees, to his feet, with his hands high in the air.

Pres found a butcher knife on the chuck wagon and freed Bob Brady. "I guess it's over," he said as he cut the ropes away. "Your sister's all right. I'm Pres Morehead, and I'll be obliged if you'll help me get this arm tied up. Are there any more of these gun artists around that you folks took pleasure in hiring?"

"No," said Bob Brady huskily. "And they're the last we'll ever hire. Kathleen had a wild idea she could find who killed Tom Morehead by buying information from that whiskey seller at Corkscrew Flat. He made her believe he could get the truth if she paid him money to hand to the right men. And then when rustlers got at our cattle, it seemed logical to have O'Leary get us some men who were ready to use their guns and keep strangers out. O'Leary sent us these men, and the rustling stopped. Yesterday Kathleen told me that a man had come asking for the Moreheads. She thought he was a law officer. I didn't know she was so worried that she'd ride over to Corkscrew Flat last night and ask O'Leary if he had information for her. He wanted more money. Kathleen took McAlister for protection on the ride, and there was a shooting outbreak while she was talking to O'Leary. Kathleen galloped home alone. She hadn't been home an hour when McAlister came to the door. Instead of explaining what had happened, he told us he was clearing out with his men, and we were going along to sell the Bar Z cattle for them."

Bob Brady paused and continued ruefully: "McAlister told us he and his men were all on the run from the law, and O'Leary had been hiding them out and helping them dispose of cattle they rustled. O'Leary told them we would hire them, and they'd be safer inside our fences drawing pay than hiding out. So they worked for us and left our cattle alone. Last night O'Leary double-crossed them in some way, and they decided to move on and take all our stock . . . and make us sell it for them." Bob

Brady licked his lips. "I didn't like the way McAlister looked at Kathleen all this morning. It's . . . it's pretty terrible to be helpless to protect someone you care for."

"I'll bet," agreed Pres. "But she's all right now. Doc Winthrop snagged her a horse. Here they come."

But Ed Safford was there first, complaining loudly as he leaped off his horse. "Pres, why didn't you shuck your hat when you seen trouble? You done us dirt and stole the fight."

Pres grinned as he stepped away from the chuck wagon to go meet Doc Winthrop and Kathleen Brady. "I'll tell you later, Ed," he promised. "Right now I've got other things to tell. I was too busy to think of them when I left the lady, but they're coming back to me now."

Ed Safford didn't get it. Wise old Doc Winthrop probably wasn't fooled, judging by the way he was smiling. As Pres limped forward, something hungry and eager that had stayed with him through the long years of exile went to that meeting with Doc Winthrop and the Brady girl, sitting her horse with the proud fire that was the expression of her spirit. Nothing that had happened in this terror-filled day had been able to quench that fire. Nothing ever would, Pres knew.

★ ★ ★ ★ ★

RIDE THE BLOOD TRAIL

★ ★ ★ ★ ★

T.T. Flynn titled this story "Take the Blood Trail", completed on August 25, 1948. He did this even though he knew it would be sent to editor Mike Tilden at Popular Publications and that Tilden was certain to change the title. It was bought in October, 1948 and the author was paid $393.00. When it appeared in *Fifteen Western Tales* (1/49) it was titled as above, this title being retained for its first appearance in book form.

I

The screaming voice was thin and far off, with terror that caught at Dave Garrison's usually cool nerves. Garrison heard it at dawn when he rode up out of the great rock-walled slash of Ghost Cañon. He had meant to roll a cigarette and rest the dun horse. Instead, he stood sharply in the stirrups, testing the brightening dawn, a close-knit, flat-flanked young man with black hair. He came back hard to the saddle and brought the rein ends whistling down. The dun horse exploded into the gallop that had made other men swear with admiring envy.

The way was littered with stunted bushes, scanty grass clumps, and lush cactus thrusting among weathered rock outcroppings. The dun raced sure-footedly through the rough going. It burst over another rise, and a screaming slug going past Garrison's shoulder came from the rocky ground pitched downward and studded with heavy cactus growth. The gunman was scrambling on a gray horse, rifle in hand. One horse. One man who had been determined to kill on sight.

Garrison yanked his handgun and the spur-raked dun hurtled on down the rough slope. The mounted figure ahead whirled the gray horse and fired a rifle shot at the ground. He levered furiously and drove more lead screaming past Garrison's elbow. Only then, as the dun rushed close, did Garrison open fire. Something in the reckless fury of his approach seemed to unnerve the gunman. He yanked the gray horse toward cover of a jagged rock outcrop.

Garrison emptied his handgun in a fast, calculated burst, and as the spurring stranger vanished behind the rocks, Garrison pulled his saddle gun without slackening speed. A rush to close quarters was as safe as hunting cover now. Others might be near to help the stranger.

Then of a sudden everything changed. The stranger's veering horse came into view again. The rider was off the saddle and a foot caught in a stirrup. The plunging, bucking gray horse was bolting away, dragging the man, bouncing and slamming, head down over the rocky ground. He might have been dead as he left the saddle. Garrison never knew. In that instant he ceased to care as the rushing dun passed the spot where the stranger had been standing.

Garrison brought the dun up sliding, rearing, snorting its own awareness of terror in the dawn. Garrison hit the ground, running. His insides were gathering, knotting. The first shafts of sunrise brushed gold on the tall spiked cactus near earthen mounds that big red ants had built, mounds above a man's knee, broad and teeming. And the ants had not waited for the golden sun. They clotted on top of the largest mound in a monstrous, seething mass, and the mass heaved slowly and screamed thinly.

Garrison snapped open a spring-blade knife and ran in at stake ropes that spread-eagled arms and legs now covered and clotted with the mass of living red. He had to step on the red carpet to reach all four ropes. Live fire spilled down inside his boots. It flowed up his wrist as he grabbed an ankle and heaved back.

He dragged the thing and all its monstrous seething red cocoon out over the clean, bare ground. He flopped it over and over, using both hands, and dragged it farther away. He snatched off his stained old black hat and beat at it savagely.

He looked at what his beating sombrero had uncovered and a

retching came up in his throat. He dragged it on away from the big ants he had knocked off. Then, a little wild himself with a kind of sweeping horror, Garrison yanked off coat, shirt, boots, and slapped and brushed and cleared his own body of the vicious fire bites.

The screaming had died away. The gunman had shot from the saddle to kill this thing that had once been a man. Perhaps so it couldn't talk. Garrison looked, long and hard, as he reloaded his handgun. He sucked in a shaking breath. His face was stony. All this was beyond pity or hesitation. For what had been a man with eyes and clean whole face still jerked spasmodically, still lived a little. A last booming shot rolled away through the dawn. Garrison hauled his clothes back on.

The dawn quiet had a brooding weight. Garrison carried the body to a big flat rock, and then rode after the gray horse.

He found the body a good mile away, where it had finally twisted free of the stirrup. The horse, reins over saddle horn, had kept on running.

Garrison kneeled by the battered corpse. It was an American. The victim on the ant hill had been Mexican. Pockets held no identification. In a heavy canvas money belt were seven double eagles.

Garrison left the stranger there without regret and put the dun horse into a long run west across the dry and broken mesa. A full hour later he came without warning to an abrupt rimrock drop, and pulled up for the quick surge of pleasure he always had at this point. Far below the rimrock in a narrow green little valley the red-tiled roof of John Farrow's big house splotched color beside the clear shallows of a small stream.

John Farrow had built in *hacienda* style around a spacious, flower-filled patio. Trees lifted between the green of irrigated gardens. Beyond the big house were a few smaller, drab outbuildings.

Garrison sat frozen and his glance went brittle and cold. A dead horse lay near the empty horse corral. In the carriage way in front of the big house a man sprawled motionlessly, face down, arms flung out.

And then another man walked slowly out of the patio entrance, reeling a little. He halted and drank from a bottle, and reeled on a few steps, and sat heavily on a blue wooden bench, and drank again.

Garrison knew that bench well. All his life he would remember that bench, and not holding a man who swilled liquor in a dawn of death. Something snapped inside. Garrison cried thickly at the dun horse and raked spurs, and rode the fine animal dangerously in a wild rush down the trail into the valley.

The man hunched on the blue bench with his bottle while the rushing dun was pulled up, rearing with flaring nostrils. His look was dull, indifferent as Garrison caught him by a shoulder, shaking him in a kind of wild fury.

The shabby little man was not armed. He showed no resentment as Garrison dragged him upright, raging: "Talk, damn you!"

Uncut iron-gray hair fell over the man's eyes as Garrison shook him. Dully he said: "I didn't kill no one. I'm Jimmy Green, heading for the railroad. Stopped here last night."

Garrison released the shoulder. "Green? Where from?"

"San Carlos Mine," said Green. He mouthed each fuzzy word carefully. He was, Garrison saw, glassy-eyed drunk, in the way of a man never sober.

"Sam Meredith's drunken bookkeeper?"

Green nodded owlishly. "The books always balanced," he said huskily. He licked his lips. "Drunk las' night . . . and it won't balance." He shivered and lifted the bottle with a convulsive movement.

Garrison hurled the bottle into the shrubbery behind the

bench. "Where's John Farrow?"

Jimmy Green jerked an unsteady thumb at the tall, carved wooden gates open at the patio entrance. "Big room to the right. No use running."

But Garrison was running. The large parlor to the right was a big dim room with carved ebony and mahogany furniture. John Farrow was there, hanging head down by roped ankles hauled up to the center of the heavy wrought-iron chandelier with its circle of glass-bowled lamps.

The room was a shambles. Broken glasses, empty bottles, cigarette and cigar ends on rugs and the smooth, waxed floor. Farrow's wrist was cold. Garrison swung back to the flowers and greenery of the patio. Jimmy Green waited there on uncertain legs. He saw the wild look Garrison cast around. Pity entered the little man's glassy look.

"Third room back, mister. But I wouldn't go in there."

Garrison bolted toward the room. He leaned the carbine beside the doorway and slowly walked inside.

Jimmy Green was on a patio bench drinking from another bottle when Garrison emerged with heavy steps and ignored the proffered bottle.

Jimmy Green whispered creakily: "There's more of them back at the servant's houses. Wasn't no one left to talk." He gulped. "A bottle don' help."

Garrison said wonderingly: "She was to have been married next month. To a good man. I rode all night to tell her I was happy . . . even if it had to be someone else." Garrison wheeled on the gray-faced little drunk. His violent question was raw with threat. "Who did it?"

"I ain't been sober in years, mister. I was drunk last night. Thought it was a dream."

"All this a dream?" demanded Garrison savagely.

"I've dreamed worse," the little man mumbled. "Snakes at

my face. Things you never seen on earth laughing and screaming in the dark. I was dead drunk in the bushes behind that
bench last night. I thought it was just another dream till I
crawled out this morning."

"What did you dream?"

Jimmy Green shivered at the memory. "When I seen what
had happened and got part of a bottle down, some of it come
back. There were shots and yells. There was a voice I thought I
knew, speaking by that blue bench. 'This 'un almost got away,
you fools! Get 'em all.' "

Garrison said explosively: "You knew his voice!"

"Thought I did. A thousand strangers come by the San Carlos
Mine. Must've been one of them. I don' know which one."

"Think, damn you."

"I been thinking. It's like a hot coal in my head. I'll never
forget that voice. But I dunno."

"You'll remember the voice?" Garrison pressed.

"Kind of sneering, it was, like it hadn't no use for anyone. I'll
know it if I ever hear it again."

Garrison reached for the bottle. It was fiery Indies rum,
double-distilled. John Farrow had been a retired sea captain. He
had shipped rum in by the case. The liquor tore at Garrison's
throat and burned deep inside, showing why Jimmy Green had
been dead drunk last night on it.

"We'll look around," said Garrison, choking a little.

John Farrow had been a strange man in a way, a watchful,
moody man of little talk. Years ago he'd found this lonely little
valley under the rimrock and had settled here. Farrow had run
no cattle, kept no crew of riders. A few Mexicans did what was
needed around the place. Here, two years ago, a niece, Marcia
Ames, had come to visit, and had stayed, bringing a new and
needed youth and gaiety. More than friendship for Marcia had
built up in Garrison. Before he'd said so, Marcia had written

she was engaged to marry another man.

This day Garrison buried her outside the big house, under the tall trees, near the murmuring little creek, and John Farrow and the others beside her.

Jimmy Green sweated, too, with pick and shovel. When it was over and the day was running out, Garrison said curtly: "I'll get you a horse. We're riding."

It was a long day's ride to the Big Hat Store, a second day's ride to Napa and the sheriff. They rode all night to the small cluster of adobe huts and one larger building that was the Big Hat Store.

Lindiger, the bulky, stolid Dutchman who owned the store, stumped out on his peg leg in the dawn as Garrison all but lifted Jimmy Green from the saddle and led him by an arm, reeling, to a box against the storefront.

An, hour later, fed, washed, shaved, gaunt, and red-eyed, Garrison climbed on a lean chestnut horse, the best the Dutchman had.

"Remember, no whiskey for Green. Not a drink," Garrison said as he gathered the reins.

"Dot kills him maybe, but I do it," promised Lindiger, and he would. The Dutchman was a stubborn man.

Two hours of daylight were left and Ike Fanning, the Napa sheriff, was still at the courthouse, when Garrison walked in on stiff legs.

Fanning took one look and came out of his chair. "Man, you look half dead."

"We buried them," Garrison finished heavily. "The one on the ant hill was Pablo Montoya, houseman for Farrow."

Fanning was a thin, rawhide sort of man, a good sheriff, and not one to back away from trouble. Some of the rock hardness, the eating grimness driving Garrison had entered the sheriff as he listened.

"Why the ant hill, so far from the house?" he wondered aloud.

"The bunch rode that way. Looks like they kept on in a hurry and left one man to watch Pablo and the ant hill. Perhaps to hear what Pablo said if he broke down and talked before he died. The fellow tried to kill him when I showed up. Tried to make sure he'd never talk, I guess."

Fanning nodded. "What do you know about John Farrow?"

"Not much. Three years ago I took over his Ventana Mine on shares. Farrow never came near the mine."

"Knew his niece pretty well, didn't you?" asked Fanning shrewdly, showing he kept in touch with gossip in his district.

"We were friends," said Garrison shortly.

"She ever talk about the years her uncle went to sea?"

"No. She never saw Farrow until two years ago. She'd written him that her mother, Farrow's sister, had died. Took almost a year to get a reply. Farrow sent money. Asked her to come on from New Orleans and visit him. He was all the family she had left. She went. I think Farrow was lonesome. Anyway, he asked Marcia to stay on, and she did."

Fanning rolled a cigarette thoughtfully. Garrison built a smoke, too. His hands were unsteady. "Starting a posse tonight?" he questioned tightly.

"No hurry," Fanning murmured. "The trail will be days old." He opened the bottom drawer of his desk and burrowed among old envelopes and papers. He straightened with a long, soiled envelope that held one folded paper. He opened the paper carefully on the desk and said mildly: "Five or six years ago I stopped in to see my old friend Alec Bart, sheriff at White Cañon, up in the Green River country. I found this in a stack of old Reward dodgers back in Alec's desk."

Garrison looked down at an old yellowed Reward notice. A corner had been torn off. The paper was brittle with age. "Five hundred reward," he read aloud. "The Rawhide Kid, murder, bank robbery, hold-up of two Union Pacific trains. Age about twenty-eight, height about five-seven. Black beard. Little finger missing from left hand. Scar at corner of left eye . . ." Garrison's voice trailed off in a slow breath. His gaze swung to Fanning's level estimation.

Fanning said: "Alec Bart guessed the dodger was put out near twenty years back. As far as Alec knew, the Rawhide Kid wasn't seen afterward." Fanning put the dodger in the envelope. He was calm. "John Farrow had built his place. Wasn't any rustling or law-breaking out that way. I dropped by for a good look at his eye scar and missing little finger, and thanked him for his grub and rode away. There's more to making a good sheriff than hunting any kind of a reason for an arrest."

"The Rawhide Kid," said Garrison slowly, trying to link that old Reward dodger with the gray-haired, silent man he'd known. With Marcia's uncle. With Marcia's family.

Fanning said: "Old Alec Bart said the Rawhide Kid had ridden with as wild a bunch of young gunnies as the territory up there had ever seen. Red Malloy, Mex Peters, Big Whitey Bell . . ."

"I've heard of Whitey Bell," said Garrison.

Fanning nodded. "A bad one. Alec said they were a young, kill-crazy bunch. But they faded out. Some were shot or hanged. Mex Peters was seen in South America. Big Whitey Bell got a life sentence for train robbery. Got religion in prison and a pardon." Fanning's grin took a wintry edge. "Big Whitey went to preaching against sin and liquor in tent meetings."

Garrison said: "Don't make sense, the Rawhide Kid ending up a sea captain."

Fanning closed the desk drawer. "Whoever heard of a sea captain settling where Farrow did? And with the money he had? No one around here ever saw him on a ship. Farrow told that story and said no more about it. He kept to himself. He had all the money he could use. It's been guessed for years that Farrow had a small fortune hidden out there at his place. Gold money, bullion bars from the two mines he'd bought."

Garrison hesitated. "Might be a little truth to it. The Ventana Mine never made anybody rich. But it made a profit. Farrow took his half in gold money. Had me bring it to him every now and then. Said he didn't like banks."

"Doesn't matter what he had hidden," said Fanning. "If folks thought he had treasure there, it's a reason for the raid on his place."

Fanning had been sheriff a long time. He was a calm, shrewd man. "We'll start in the morning," he decided. "That's soon enough, seeing as you buried everyone."

II

Garrison was like a dead man in the hotel bed when Fanning hammered on the door. They were six as they rode toward the Big Hat Store. One was the chief deputy, Slack Summers. And there was Yuma Charley, short and broad, with an Indian cast to his features, sandy hair and freckled, sun-reddened face—his father a Scotsman, mother part Yaqui, part Mexican.

"I keep a pack outfit at the Dutchman's store," Fanning told Garrison. "Slack Summers and the others can do what's needed at Farrow's place. I'll trail on from there with Yuma Charley. He can follow sign like it was printed."

Garrison was a better man after the night's sleep. A somber hardness had settled on him.

"You and a half-breed tracker going to bring in that bunch?" he asked with irony.

"I want an idea where they're heading."

"Then what?"

"I'll think about it."

"Make me a deputy," urged Garrison abruptly. "Kind of arrest this Jimmy Green as a suspicious witness, and let me take charge of him. I'll put him on the Ventana payroll, so his time won't be wasted."

Fanning's alertness sharpened. "Why should I?"

"Call it a favor."

"I want a reason."

Garrison rode in hard and bitter silence for a moment. "I'm going after them," he said briefly.

"Because of the girl?"

"She was no part of Farrow's past," said Garrison, not aware of the clubbing harshness in his voice. "She'd just made a trip back to Louisiana. Promised to marry a fine young fellow back there. She was back for a last visit with Farrow." Garrison's neck muscles corded as he swallowed hard. "I had to bury her. I've got to write the man who's waiting for her. Then I mean to see grave dirt go on the men who raided that place. She killed herself, but they drove her to it."

Fanning said—"I'll think about it."—and rode on ahead to side his chief deputy.

They reached Big Hat before dark. Ike Fanning talked to Jimmy Green alone. Later, as night struck, Jimmy Green asked Garrison to step outside the store. The little San Carlos book-keeper was twitching from raw nerves and need of a drink.

"Sheriff says you've got a job that'll keep me out of jail as a witness."

"That's right."

"I got to have a drink now! That damned Dutchman won't open a bottle!"

"No drinks."

"I'll die!"

"If the sheriff locks you up, there won't be any booze. Try to ride away for some now and I'll help Fanning bring you back," Garrison said bluntly.

Jimmy Green groaned as he turned away.

They made Farrow's place early the next afternoon. The big house was as Garrison had left it, peaceful, quiet. It was the brooding quiet of blasted hopes, of dreams destroyed. The quiet of death.

Fanning spent less than an hour looking around and examining John Farrow's looted desk. Then he rode toward Ghost Cañon with his half-breed tracker. Garrison and Jimmy Green went along. From the high rimrock, Garrison looked back down at the little valley and the blue bench, resting empty before the patio entrance.

He'd sat on that bench with Marcia Ames. He could see the newly spaded dirt where he'd buried her within sight of the bench. His features were stony as he reined on after the others.

Fanning had a shovel lashed to his pack. They hurriedly buried the two dead men out on the wild mesa.

Yuma Charley, cigarette hanging on his lip, walked about the area in stolid silence. "I think seven men come this way. Two pack horses," Yuma Charley decided. "Too much start. Damn' long trail ahead."

Shod hoof tracks led them toward Ghost Cañon. In sight of the cañon Yuma Charley hauled up. "Two riders, one pack horse go into cañon." Charley swung an arm north. "Others that way."

Ike Fanning squinted into the north. "They'll go off the mesa into the salt hills and leave sign at Ox Head Spring. We'll go that way. Good luck, Garrison."

They parted in that casual manner, death behind them, death ahead. Men who had raided John Farrow's place and staked Farrow's man out on an ant hill wouldn't take chances with anyone who came up with them.

The last sunlight was on the high sky as Garrison took the tortuous down path into the pooling shadows deep in Ghost Cañon. He saw now where the two riders had turned up the cañon. He led Jimmy Green down the cañon toward the Ventana Mine.

Past midnight they reached the mine, dark and quiet now, with no night shift working. Jimmy Green fell on a cot in Garrison's little three-room adobe house close to the mine office. He was twitching, groaning as his whiskey-soaked body demanded liquor. He came up with a groaning cry when Garrison shook him awake in the morning.

Mike Shaughnessy, the mine foreman, was a hard-headed Irishman who broke six feet barefooted. Shaughnessy's deep voice could come soft as a woman's tone or blast in a roar of rage. This morning Shaughnessy stood approvingly in front of the mine office while Garrison tested the pack rope, and Jimmy Green, in a new canvas saddle jacket and pants and riding boots, drooped shakily in the saddle.

"I'll say it again, if it costs me my job," said Mike Shaughnessy bluntly. "Stay here where you belong and work out the devils that are stomping your heart."

"Damn your loose mouth, Mike," Garrison said softly. "Keep it closed."

"I've said it," Shaughnessy grumbled. His voice took a soft understanding, a little wistful. "When a man rides into the fire, only the good God knows whether he'll be burnt or purified. It's big game you're hunting." And to the unsteady little bookkeeper, Shaughnessy said, somewhat maliciously: "If you find a whiskey spring, bring it back."

Jimmy Green rode off cursing the big grinning Ventana foreman.

That night they camped far up Ghost Cañon with the shod tracks pointing onward. Jimmy Green cried out wildly now and then in his twitching sleep.

Late next afternoon they followed the tracks out of the cañon on the little-used Black Sheep Mesa trail. And far out on the fantastic, eroded waste of mesa, the shod tracks split. Pack horse and one rider swung off to the left. Here the two men had dismounted, sat down, and drained a bottle of Farrow's fiery rum. The bottle was dry inside. Jimmy Green hurled it against a rock in frantic disappointment.

Garrison was searching for sign. One man had rolled tobacco in brown paper. He left several fat cigarette ends, rolled larger than most men cared to smoke. Garrison picked up two and studied them, and then dropped them and decided: "We'll follow the pack horse. That one will travel slower."

Nine days later they were on the same trail. Yuma Charley could not have held the sign better than the somber, fierce persistence that pushed Garrison on day after day. On rocky stretches where a man could only guess, he circled far out, patiently, until the tracks showed again. He combed each camp site with fierce persistence that would not be denied.

His knowledge of the man ahead slowly grew. A horse had rolled and left several black hairs. The man had shaved, and tiny clumps of dried soap on the ground held yellow face bristles. The man chewed black twist. He'd shot a rattler at one camp and left a .44 six-gun shell. He was a tall man by the length of his stride prints. He put his horses on stake ropes and hobbled them, too. Garrison found roan horse hairs at one picket spot. So the man had a black horse and a roan horse. He had killed rattlers, and often shot the heads off neatly. He was a dead shot.

More of John Farrow's empty bottles appeared along the trail. The man liked liquor. He drank as he rode. Some of the bottles had been emptied and tossed away without stopping. Each time they found a dry bottle, Jimmy Green cursed in disappointment. But the little San Carlos bookkeeper was changing. He'd stopped shaking. He began to sleep soundly. Appetite grew. Sun and wind took the gray look off his face. He sat in the saddle straighter and complained less as the whiskey worked out of his flesh and a new strength crept in.

They crossed the great Sour Water badlands, into country Garrison knew only by hearsay, on into the shale slopes of the Pendero foothills, up into the pines of the higher Penderos, always far from settlements and ranches. The renegade traveled fast and trail wise. He made halts on the high points, smoking his fat brown paper cigarettes and evidently studying the back trail patiently for sign of pursuit.

They came off more mountains, down an old sheep trail, and crossed a deep, narrow cañon on a rickety swing bridge floored with loose, sun-warped planks. White water tearing at the black rocks far below boomed up at them. The hoof marks of two horses led onto the bridge—and only one horse came off. Garrison pulled up, puzzling it out, studying the growling depths below. Trying to read the stranger's thoughts at this point.

Jimmy Green rode back. "Something's wrong?"

"He led his pack horse on the bridge . . . and came off the bridge without it," said Garrison. He rolled a smoke and lit it and decided: "I'm not sure where we are. But he is. He wants to ride light now, like he hasn't been packing on a long trail."

They came off the heights, down out of the aspens and pines, down to a valley road, and the sign vanished, churned away under iron-tired wagon wheels and recent passings of horses and cattle.

"He counted on this," Garrison guessed. He shaped another cigarette and murmured: "A tall man with yellow hair, riding a black or a roan horse. Tobacco in his cheek or a fat brown paper cigarette in his face. He likes liquor. He won't pass a saloon. Might buy some Forty-Four shells for his six-shooter."

Jimmy Green said thinly: "Where?"

Garrison said: "Let's find out."

The first little sheep settlement had no word of a tall yellow-haired man. But forty miles down the widening valley at Flat Rock, a bald-headed barber talked above the lather on Garrison's face. "Long-legged, yellow-haired stranger? One like that was in here for a shave and a trim. Had a bath, too. Said he was a cattle buyer from Kansas City."

A fat hotel clerk with pink sleeve bows and thinning hair remembered the yellow-haired man. He'd signed the register as Bud Corrigan. Had put up his black saddle horse at the feed barn around the corner, a tall, taciturn, yellow-haired man with a new-sprouting yellow mustache. Corrigan had a black leather gun belt, worn riding boots, denim trousers and jacket. He'd drunk whiskey at two bars, turned in early, left Flat Rock at daybreak, not saying where he was heading.

"We'll try north," Garrison decided with cold patience. "He's been heading that way."

There was a kind of relentless, terrible patience in the way Garrison followed. They lost the trail at Flat Rock. Garrison cast out to new roads, new trails. Jimmy Green, saddle-hardened and increasingly resentful, argued: "You aim to keep on like this?"

Garrison nodded somberly. He said—"It's not hurting you."—and extended his steady hand. After a moment Jimmy Green did the same. His hand was steady, too.

"I know," the little man admitted. "That's why I'm staying with you. I'd have a whiskey bottle at the first bar I hit alone." He rode glumly. "We're death riding to meet death," he said. "You know it. We won't get back."

Garrison said: "What difference?"

Jimmy Green let it stand. Neither had bright memories calling back there in the far south.

They rode into a widening valley, into another little town, Talus by name. Just another town, with a run of silver dust on its main street. The Drover's Palace Hotel was a two-story frame with carpeted stairs and a chipped iron bedstead and well-worn chairs in the front room they took. The usual assortment of stores flanked the dusty street. The sun had a brassy strike as Garrison started the round of casual questions about a long-legged, yellow-haired stranger. It was like casting a hook into unknown pools and always drawing it back empty. But casting, casting. . . . Jimmy Green joined him and they turned in under a sign that said: *Jason Mckay, General Mdse.*

They were the only customers at the moment. The girl who stepped to wait on them was smiling.

"I'd like a handkerchief, please, ma'am," Garrison said, and found himself smiling, too. His first real smile of the trip.

She said: "Over here, please." The tap of her heels to a showcase had a lightness of youth and spirit.

She put out neckerchiefs in cotton and silk, in red, blue, black. Her small hands were deft. Interest lighted her sun-dusted face. She had tawny hair that needed the wind in it, Garrison thought. He said—"Hard to make a choice."—and waited expectantly for her light chuckle.

It came, and she suggested: "Why not buy one of each kind?"

Garrison chuckled, too, whole-heartedly, and missed the astonished lift of Jimmy Green's sun-bleached eyebrows. She might be twenty, Garrison guessed, a slim and generous-mouthed girl who gave him a lift of spirits he'd forgotten.

Beyond a line of washtubs hanging from a wire-suspended board, other voices sounded in a back storeroom, one louder, sneeringly impatient. "For fifty dollars less, I could have my pick of better horses anywhere in town!"

Jimmy Green's sunburned hand on the showcase closed convulsively. Garrison forgot handkerchiefs and the girl as he saw Jimmy Green standing, taut and fearful. The little man's head jerked in assent that changed Garrison to a coldly functioning instrument.

Garrison said: "I'll take a blue one, ma'am." And to Jimmy Green: "You'd better tend to that business back at the hotel."

Jimmy Green almost scurried to the door.

The girl was puzzled as she wrapped the handkerchief. She looked after Jimmy Green. Her blue eyes rested on Garrison's chiseled face. He tried to bring back the smiling moment. "Sounds like a sharp horse trade back there, ma'am."

"Dad won't be out-traded," she remarked confidentially. "He's not too anxious to sell. Mase Bragdon just happened to bring the man in."

"And who is Mase Bragdon?"

She said: "You're a stranger, too, aren't you? Mase is the sheriff's son. Tom Bragdon's son."

"And the stranger?"

"I don't know. Mase brought him in."

She laid the small flat package on the counter. Garrison paid her and waited while she went back to an under-counter cash drawer for his change.

Garrison's unobtrusive glance raked three men who came out of the back room. The black cloth sleeve guards would be on Jason McKay, the girl's father. He was a thin, erect, briskly-moving man with a still-tawny mustache. Mase Bragdon, younger than Garrison would have guessed from his heavy voice, was a burly young fellow, a cocky angle to his gray hat, a satisfied smile on his smooth-shaven face. A double-gun young fellow with a swagger. The third man was the horse buyer, the stranger whose voice had struck Jimmy Green cold with memory. That one had a tough, old-leather look. Medium-built, he had a long, thin nose, a grizzled mustache on a narrow face, and a mouth almost wolf-like in faintly sneering arrogance. Another double-gun man. A lean, dangerous oldster. What did not show about him Garrison already knew, after this man and his friends had ridden away from John Farrow's place.

The three men entered a cluttered, glassed-in office enclosure at the back corner of the store. The girl returned with change, smiling. "I thought Mase would buy that horse. He came home only last week. If he's going to stay deputy under his father, he'll need a good horse."

Garrison stood with change in one hand, package in the other. "Where's Mase Bragdon been?" he questioned idly.

She laughed softly. "To hear Mase tell it, everywhere. He hasn't been back for more than a few days at a time in years."

Garrison knew she watched him out of the store. Another time he would have stayed, as a thirsty man lingers by sparkling water. Jimmy Green had locked the hotel room door. Garrison sailed the flat handkerchief package to the bed.

"He isn't the man we've been following. Looks like a bad-acting old lobo wolf. Scar up the side of his neck, behind the ear."

"Neck scar." Jimmy Green's head bobbed in sudden remembrance. "That neck-scarred stranger stopped at the San Carlos Mine a few months ago. Prospecting, he said. Name was . . . Carter. That's it, Windy Carter."

"Any name will do," said Garrison shortly. He was checking his six-gun. "Young fellow named Mase Bragdon, the sheriff's son, is with him." Garrison's look was hard with speculation. "Young Bragdon's been away for years. Just back. I wonder where he was the night John Farrow was murdered?"

Jimmy Green's mouth was open soundlessly and Garrison considered him soberly. "You recognized the voice. Now you better head out to the railroad after dark." Jimmy Green had a drawn and worried look as he nodded.

Behind screening peaks, far from the railroad, Talus was a small but solid town, gateway to the back mountain country. Wagon and stage traffic, trade and strangers made Talus prosperous. Garrison pondered all that as he had a shave at a barbershop and moved on for casual drinks and talk in the saloons.

He had a tight feeling of danger. On the long trail danger had been ahead. Always ahead. Now any man he stood beside at a bar might be danger. News of the raid on Farrow's ranch had spread. It had been printed in distant weekly newspapers. Here in Talus, Garrison heard a bearded rancher speak of it over a beer bottle.

"Wonder if they found out who shot up that ranch house near Napa?"

And now young Mase Bragdon was friendly with the lean, wolf-like oldster who'd left his voice and neck scar in Jimmy Green's drunken memory. Garrison looked for a tall, yellow-haired man with a fat brown paper cigarette. Others of that renegade gang might have visited the Ventana Mine and been familiar with Dave Garrison's face. Already he might have been recognized. It made Garrison coldly wary of any man who looked his way.

He saw the burly figure of Mase Bragdon turn into a small frame building across the street that housed the weekly Talus *Times*. Garrison built a cigarette and crossed to the newspaper office. The smell of paper and printer's ink met him inside. A red-headed girl, tall and lithe, left her table desk and came to the counter. Mase Bragdon sat beside her table and weighed the stranger.

"I'm a stranger, ma'am," said Garrison mildly. "Would the paper know of any bargain land for sale not too far from town?"

She said lightly: "The *Times* knows everything." Her glance went over to Mase Bragdon. "Mase, are you thinking of selling that Moose Creek place your mother left you? Or won't you know until you take Nancy McKay to the dance tonight?"

Mase grinned. "That's somethin' for the paper to find out, Alma." He came to the counter. "Where you from, mister?"

"Texas. The Big Bend," said Garrison in some truth. He'd been in the wild Big Bend country at one time.

"I rode through there," said Mase Bragdon. "Camped at Dry Well store, run by that one-legged Mexican named Sanchez. Know him?"

"Dry Well store is run by old Comanch' Walker, the one-eyed old hellion."

Mase Bragdon grinned. "Got my stores mixed. You're right."

He came through the counter gate. "Alma has got to look for some news to print. She won't be interested in our talk." He left Alma irritated, and enjoyed it. But when they turned along the walk, Mase Bragdon said bluntly: "I got a small place I'll sell cheap in a quick cash trade."

Garrison had entered the newspaper office on the chance of idle talk with the sheriff's burly son. He hadn't looked for this. But he said: "Sounds good. Let's ride out and see your place."

Mase Bragdon hesitated. "Tomorrow," he decided. "I seen you in McKay's store. Fellow I was with is looking for a small ranch, too. Only his cash ain't so quick. The place is yours, mister, if you like it tomorrow."

"Got to be a real bargain."

"It will be."

After young Bragdon left him, Garrison sat in a weathered splint rocker on the hotel verandah, and considered. Mase Bragdon had been home a few days. Talus folks thought he meant to settle down, but Mase Bragdon didn't think so. Wouldn't be offering his land cheap, for a quick sale, if he meant to settle down. And Bragdon was taking Nancy McKay to a dance tonight.

A man came by wearing the sheriff's badge. Garrison leaned forward a little, studying Tom Bragdon, the sheriff. He was big, like his son, stooping a little, hair white, deep lines on his face, as if he had had his share of worry. A big, placid man, this sheriff, with none of his son's swagger, but with a solidness that suggested that the sheriff's badge was worn by a good man.

Alma, the redhead, came briskly along the walk and spoke with the sheriff. Both stood smiling, and when Alma came on, she stopped at the low verandah rail, an arm's reach away. Her smile had a different quality, an anxiety. "Did you buy the ranch? The *Times* likes to print everything."

"Nice town," said Garrison readily. "Nice folks. Pretty girls. Any man would like to settle around here."

Her hat was small and perky. She was pretty and she knew it. Her mouth was ripe and her gray-greenish eyes challenging. She said: "So Mase is thinking of selling?"

Garrison's grin told her nothing. "Ask Mase at the dance tonight," he suggested.

"I'm not going to the dance."

Garrison leaned forward, not sure why he said: "I'd be honored, ma'am, if you'd consider going to the dance with me."

She was startled. Garrison guessed she was not as bold as her ripe mouth and greenish-gray eyes suggested. He watched purpose come to her. "I'll go," she decided.

Jimmy Green was pacing the hotel room nervously when Garrison walked in.

"I'm staying in town," the little San Carlos bookkeeper said half defiantly.

Garrison peered at the smaller man. "Why?"

Jimmy Green muttered: "A man can't keep running from himself. I saw what you saw at Farrow's ranch. Heard some of it. I guess I got to stay." He swallowed hard. "What do we do?"

Garrison's smile was slow and warming. "You're a better man than started with me. But keep out of sight. I'm taking a lady to a dance tonight."

"That girl at the store?"

"No. From the paper. A redhead. And don't ask me why. I'm

not sure myself," said Garrison a little sheepishly.

That evening at the schoolhouse with his pretty red-headed partner, Garrison knew he'd come because Nancy McKay would be here. And he was uneasy already. Alma Stevens had said there'd be no guns at the dance, and he'd left cartridge belt and six-shooter at her house. Garrison had a feeling he shouldn't have come, not in Talus, not without his gun. This was a middle-of-the-week dance, gotten up by friends on Nancy's twenty-first birthday. When Garrison walked in with Alma Stevens, his first thought was that Nancy was the prettiest girl on the dance floor. Her tawny hair was caught back and her blue eyes were sparkling.

Mase Bragdon, in gray broadcloth and black string tie, was dancing with Nancy. Garrison felt Alma Stevens's hand tighten on his arm. He caught a shadow of unhappiness in her eyes. "Mase is a fine dancer," Alma said, and Garrison felt sorry for her. She wanted Mase Bragdon and Mase had another girl.

Pine branches and flowers decorated the room. This was Talus enjoying itself away from the saloons. Garrison hadn't been in such neighborly fun in a long time. None of the men wore guns. The edge of Garrison's uneasiness dulled.

Mase Bragdon grinned when he saw Garrison and his partner. Mase didn't seem to mind, or to mind who danced with Nancy McKay, either. Presently he vanished. Later Garrison saw him coming in from the back with a flush on his heavy face. Mase Bragdon came over, grinning. He smelled of whiskey.

"Step out back an' grab a snort, mister."

"Might do it," Garrison assented.

Mase wiped a hand across his mouth. "I'm still dry." He went out back again.

Garrison was waiting his chance at Nancy McKay's side alone. He caught it and smiled down at her. "Your birthday party is nice, ma'am."

"I'm glad you could come with Alma." Nancy had been glowing. She sobered now. "I saw Mase come in. He's drinking, and the Bragdon men always get mean when they drink." She looked around. "Alma Stevens might talk him out of it."

"He came with you, ma'am," suggested Garrison.

"Mase's folks have always lived next door. When Mase quarreled with Alma, he was nice to me to get back at her. Alma and I are used to it," Nancy said absently.

"I thought Bragdon had settled down with a steady girl," Garrison murmured.

"Mase is fiddle-footed. Alma knows it, but she wants to believe he might settle down this time. There she is. I'll get her. . . ."

The girls came to him. Alma Stevens had a determined look. "Tell Mase to come in," she requested firmly.

Garrison went because misery lurked in her eyes, and because Nancy McKay wasn't Mase Bragdon's girl, after all.

Out back of the schoolhouse, he was blind for a moment in the starry night. A voice said: "Here's a jug. If you git too happy an' git throwed out, it's your hard luck." Chuckles came from other men standing around. Cigarette ends were glowing. The back door spewed light briefly as another man came out.

Garrison tilted the wicker-covered jug on his bent arm and made a show of drinking. He passed the jug to the newcomer, and peered around at the dark figures. "Mase Bragdon here?"

"Mase went off," he was answered. "Fellow rode up an' called Mase over for a talk. Mase come back for another drink an' walked away."

"Who talked with Bragdon?"

"A long-legged stranger. Yellow mustache. I seen him in the light from the side windows. Black horse."

"Sheriff's business," Garrison guessed.

Alma Stevens gave him an inquiring look when he came in alone. Something in his manner made her intent.

"Bragdon was called away, ma'am. And I've just remembered some business I must see to." Garrison made a helpless gesture. "I shouldn't have asked you to come."

Alma said calmly: "Can you take me home?"

Garrison had rented a rig. On the short drive, Alma asked only one sober question. "Do you really expect to buy Mase's land?"

"I don't know what I'll do," said Garrison truthfully.

"So he does want to sell," said Alma under her breath. She sat quietly in a kind of resignation, and Garrison guessed she was putting away long-lived hopes about Mase Bragdon.

Only when he stepped from her door with his gun belt's comforting weight around his middle did Garrison relax a little.

Under the smoky lantern in the livery stable, the hostler commented: "You didn't stay out long." He was an unshaven ancient with a few tooth snags and a cheek packed with tobacco. He put the hire money in a long leather purse and gossiped: "Had a stranger in tonight with a black horse and a yellow mustache. Friend o' yours?"

"I'd have to see him."

The hostler grinned. "He aimed to put his horse up. Then he seen your partner's horse. He took the lantern off the nail and studied the brand. Asked if there was a JF brand around here and who rode the horse in. Took a look at that dun horse of your'n, too. Said he'd be back later and rode on."

A man could live with a fact until he forgot it. Garrison had roped one of John Farrow's horses for Jimmy Green the day they ridden away from the newly dug graves. The brand hadn't seemed to matter until now. "I'll saddle my horse," Garrison decided.

He left the hostler very curious. The stony look was chiseled back on his face as he rode out to find the sheriff. And his mind jumped back to Ike Fanning and Yuma Charley, wondering where they were.

The sheriff's small white house was dark and the courthouse was dark, too. Garrison turned along Main Street, looking for the stranger with the yellow mustache, or Mase Bragdon, or the sheriff.

He saw a shaded lamp burning in the newspaper office. Alma was writing at her table desk when Garrison stepped in. She wore the same white party dress of soft, watered silk and must have come directly here from her house, restless and disturbed. She faced him across the counter, explaining: "I thought I'd write a piece about the dance."

Garrison nodded and asked: "Seen Mase or his father? I can't seem to find them."

"Is something wrong?"

"What could be wrong?" Garrison parried.

Alma knew he evaded and she hesitated, searching his face.

"A rancher out toward Moose Creek noticed smoke coming from the chimney of the old Bragdon house out there. He stopped here and wondered if someone was living there now. I asked Tom Bragdon. He said squatters might be using the house and he'd ride out that way after supper and see."

"Mase knew his father rode out there?"

"I don't think so."

"I'll ride that way and meet the sheriff," Garrison said. "Mind telling me how to go?"

Jimmy Green had the door of their hotel room locked. "I saw you ride up," the little man said when he let Garrison in. "I've been sitting at the front window in the dark. I've seen a tall fellow with a yellow mustache come by on a black horse."

"I know." Garrison nodded. He caught his Winchester from a room corner and checked it. "We made one mistake. That JF

brand on your horse. Yellow Mustache saw it at the stable. He
didn't have to guess why that brand was in Talus. Keep your
door locked."

"I'll go with you," said Jimmy Green at once. He had a shaky,
strained look.

"Stay here," Garrison insisted. "I'm riding to Moose Creek
to find the sheriff. It's his move. I'll give him his chance."

Garrison scanned the shadows closely as he rode out of town.
He was the hunted now, and only aware of it because he'd
taken a red-headed girl to a dance. The deck was stacked, and
the two jokers were Mase Bragdon and Tom Bragdon, the
sheriff. Tom Bragdon might have ridden to the Moose Creek
place from curiosity—or he might have carried a warning.

The night had a wind-stroked coolness, with chunks of clouds
drifting under the spattered stars. The dun's long run flung its
dust-muffled tattoo into the lonely dark. After some miles
Garrison swung left off the main stage road into a narrower
way, snaking through the first rough foothills.

Alma had said the Bragdon place was a rough bit of foothill
graze with the first mountains piling behind it. Garrison hoped
to meet the returning sheriff, but did not. He rode finally down
a pitch of road to the brawling water of Moose Creek and followed tree-dotted meadows upstream. Brush had taken the old
ranch road. Small gullies had chewed down the pitching wheel
ruts.

Alma Stevens had warned of a wire gate in the brush almost
a mile from the house. It was there, closed. Garrison stepped
down and led his horse through. A light wind rustled through
the tall brush. Coyotes were clamoring along the ridge crests.
The horse nickered and Garrison looked sharply ahead.

He froze as a command rasped at his left: "Git 'em up or git
shot!"

The man was close and invisible in the murky tangle of brush.

Garrison had a flash of agonizing indecision. It could be Sheriff Tom Bragdon, scouting the property, with a right to question an intruder. Blasting a shot in reply could be the greatest mistake Dave Garrison ever made. If he killed the Talus sheriff, he'd change from Ike Fanning's deputy to an outlaw. If the sheriff's leveled gun shot him down, all the hard patience of the long trail was wasted.

Garrison's frozen moment was the price for living inside the law. His chance passed. He lifted hands, shoulder level.

III

Brush crackled and Garrison had the truth of it. They came at him from front and back. Two men. The one who'd had a six-gun cocked in the brush at his back was the wolf-like oldster who'd bought Jason McKay's horse. He caught Garrison's gun from the holster and whipped the barrel to the side of Garrison's face, cursing as Garrison staggered.

"This one come with that JF horse. And easing out here at us already. I got a mind to blow his damn' brains all over the bushes."

He said it without much anger, as he'd shoot a rattler. But the other one was younger and sharply nervous.

"Take him to the house. We got to git holt of what he knows!"

"We'll get it. They ain't no ant hills around here, but when he sees grease roasting outta his bare feet, he'll get talky. Get his rifle, bring my horse, and then shut that gate and watch it."

Garrison climbed his saddle and wiped the blood dripping from his chin against his shoulder. His head felt like it had been split open. He was still dizzy and he had small hope. The long trail had started in death and was ending in death. A rope loop pulled tight around his middle was dallied to the saddle horn of the grizzled gunman who sided him with a gun cocked and oaths and questions driving at him.

"Where'd you come from? What's your name? Who else is around here from the south?"

"Go to hell," said Garrison, and thought for a minute he'd get shot. He wasn't.

The Bragdon house had a dark, deserted look. Windows were boarded up, warped clapboards falling away. Wild brush grew up against the house. The man with the gun on Garrison gave two short, sharp whistles. A dim figure with a shotgun stepped out of the brush. The front door flung open as Garrison dismounted and stepped out of the rope loop.

The big, white-haired man who came out of the house, gun in hand, called: "Who is it?" When he heard, his oaths were tremendous and blistering. His rolling voice was rich with satisfaction. "Bring the misguided black sheep in. We'll baptize the sin outta him till hell won't have him."

Lanterns lit a front room to the right of the doorway. An old warped kitchen table held whiskey bottles, a water bucket, tin cups, and greasy tin plates. Tom Bragdon, the sheriff, was tied in one of the chairs and watched by a lean brown gunman with white hair and a strong Mexican cast.

Tom Bragdon was puzzled by the bloody-faced prisoner. "I seen you in town. What'n hell are you doing in this?"

Garrison said: "Deputy sheriff trailing the bunch who wiped out the Farrow Ranch." And as Bragdon's mouth dropped open, Garrison said: "How come they're meeting in your town and your house?"

It hit the graying sheriff like a blow. Yellow Mustache walked in, tall and leathery, and older than Garrison had guessed. A fat brown paper cigarette was on his lip and he poured a tin cup of whiskey while he looked Garrison over.

"Deputy, huh?" he said tersely. "Where's the other one?"

"We'll git him." The big white-haired man said it as he poured whiskey, too. Hard riding had thinned him until skin hung in folds on his heavy face. He gulped a big drink and gestured at Garrison with the tin cup. "The Lord delivered the skunk to our mercies."

Yellow Mustache said: "Stop spoutin' that Bible talk. Gits on my nerves."

"The hell with your nerves, Red. I've talked that way so much it comes natural."

Garrison reached for a drink. They let him. He lowered the cup and grinned. "That mealy-mouthed talk got Whitey Bell out of prison and put fat on his belly while he preached on sin and booze along the tent meeting trail. But the Rawhide Kid never took it up, did he?"

The big white-haired man's tin cup bounced clattering on the table. His fast-drawn Colt covered Garrison. "What'n hell do you know about the Rawhide Kid?"

Tom Bragdon looked dazed as all four gunmen were startled into tense anger.

"You hauled the Kid up by his heels but you didn't get his money," Garrison guessed. "Not even staking his Mexican on an ant hill did any good." Garrison looked around at them and shook his head. "The Rawhide Kid and Whitey Bell, Mex Peters, Red Malloy, and others of the old bunch were all forgotten. But the Kid settled down with money. And the rest of the bunch who weren't hanged came at him like wolves, fanging their own pack. Damned well served you right you rode away empty-handed."

Big Whitey Bell bellowed in rage. "The Kid should 'a' been staked on that damn' ant hill. He died on me afore I got started with him, damn his thievin' heart. He dug up our money and run out on us. I might 'a' stayed outta prison with some of that money. He left us busted and got clean outta the country. While I rotted in that cell, I prayed on my knees every night to git out and find the Kid. I never stopped lookin' for a man with his little finger shot off. The other boys kept lookin', too. We finally found him and come to collect. And he died laughin' at his old partners while I prayed with him to git right with his conscience and give back that money he stole from us."

Garrison said disgustedly: "Don't talk to me about praying. I saw what your bunch left at his place. A pack of murdering hogs ran wild that night."

Windy Carter's laugh was malicious. "Whitey, he sure read the sign. We aimed to get rich again and we had to scatter and run, same as we done after the Kid cleaned us out. We figured even the old-timers had forgot us, and now they're on our trail, just like in the old days. All these years and they ain't forgot us." Windy said it with pride out of the long past. He was one of the wild young kill-crazy bunch from the Green River country—now old, grizzled, and even more dangerous.

Silence dropped as voices sounded outside. Guns were out as Mase Bragdon's burly bulk came hurriedly into the room. "So Garrison came snooping . . ."

Mase broke off at sight of his father tied in the old straight-backed chair. He gulped hard. Tom Bragdon had been silent. He sat silent now, staring at his son.

Whitey Bell grinned sourly. "Garrison ain't the only one come snooping. Thought you said no one bothered this place."

Mase went to a whiskey bottle and drank straight from the neck. "It's my place," he said sullenly, slapping the bottle down. "How'd I know the old man'd come here?" He glowered at Garrison. "Sent him out here, did you?"

Tom Bragdon spoke then evenly: "Mase, were you with these men when they murdered everyone at the JF Ranch?"

Mase said dazedly: "They done that?" He swung to Whitey Bell. "That ain't right, is it?"

"It ain't your business," said Whitey Bell shortly. "You was with Windy and Mex and the others on plenty rustlin'." Whitey

Bell reached for the bottle.

"Rustling is only rustling," said Mase thickly. "I thought . . ."

Whitey Bell lowered the bottle and gave the burly younger man a cold look. "You thought we come in here to hole up and plan a little rustlin' over acrost the mountains. And you'd be sportin' your deputy's badge an' workin' with us. But we changed our minds. Before we move on tomorrow, we'll take all the cash in that damn' bank in town, an' your old man can cover up for us."

Mase spoke with a hoarse note. "He won't do that."

"Then we'll stuff him under the dirt afore we ride to town tomorrow," said Whitey Bell roughly. "You never had no use for him nohow. I mind you told the boys you couldn't stand it at home, which is why you cut and run when you was a button. No mother and a old man who whaled hell outta you."

Tom Bragdon muttered: "I tried to be a mother and a father . . . guess I missed it all around." His eyes came up, watching Mase. "So you turned out a thief?"

"I ain't the only one who ever rustled," said Mase sullenly.

"You're the only Bragdon who ever did."

Windy said with his thin-lipped arrogance: "The hell with rustlin'! We got deputies from Napa to settle, and money to draw outta the bank in the mornin'! Mase, you're a thief like the rest of us. Don't git mealy-faced. We're lettin' you off from the bank job, so you kin use that badge to mess up the posse that'll try to foller us. It's that or you get hung for a damn' rustler! If they get you back on the Frío, enough dirt will be laid on you to drag that big neck out like a bullwhacker's whip."

"A sinner gits his pay in death, even if his pappy is a sheriff," said Whitey Bell, grinning coldly. "We'll leave your old man tied up here. You and the posse can find him tomorrow after we've smoked acrost the mountains. There's sure as hell to be someone kilt tomorrow. So if he opens his mouth, he'll be hangin' his own flesh and blood."

Tom Bragdon sat watching his son. He had no expression. Mase jerked his head at Garrison. "What about this one?"

"He's a damn' depity who's been trailin' us. I aim to kill him tonight."

Sweat glistened on Mase Bragdon's face as he looked at Garrison.

"Don't worry about me," said Garrison with a kind of savage contempt.

Mase reddened. "I ain't worrying about a stranger who comes lying to me about buying my land."

That hit Tom Bragdon hard, too. "You were dickering to sell this place your mother left you, Mase?"

"It's mine, ain't it?"

"She said so, Mase. You were born in the back bedroom there. She thought you were the finest baby any mother ever had." Tom Bragdon looked down at the floor. "What she left you is yours," he said quietly, and did not look up as Whitey Bell's impatient oath ripped out.

"We're talkin' bank money, not babies. How about it, Mase? The boys was good enough to rustle with. Now they got to get a cash stake and move on. You aim to help?"

Mase slopped whiskey into a tin cup. "I mean to ride after you," he said thickly. "The old man'll hang me like a stranger. I know him. Ask him."

Tom Bragdon spoke heavily. He sounded like a sick man. "Don't waste talk asking. My son knows me . . . and now I know my son."

Mase gulped his whiskey. He tossed the cup on the table and shoved his hat to a cocky angle. "I'll ride back to town and cry about it."

Whitey Bell differed flatly. "You ain't gittin' drunk in town tonight. Ride in after daylight and lay low. When hell busts loose, hold the posse back. We'll do the rest. Been through it plenty in the old days."

"Suppose I can't hold 'em back?" Mase was surly.

Windy spat on the floor. "Then hang back yourself. First ones close gits lead first."

Garrison was watching Tom Bragdon. It was not pleasant to see a good man die inside. Gunfire brought quick death—clean death. But Tom Bragdon's heart, pride, and long-built hopes were dying in slow misery. He'd lost his wife and lived for his son, hoping like Alma Stevens had hoped. Now Tom Bragdon had the truth.

Windy Carter stepped to Garrison's shoulder, holding a bone-handled Colt. "We got a depity waitin'." His thin grin held anticipation.

"Hold off," ordered Whitey Bell. "I got an idea. Red brought the news about the JF horse. Garrison has talked out what we need to know." Whitey Bell moved over for more whiskey. "The Book says justice oughts be mixed with mercy."

"There you go again," said Windy disgustedly.

Whitey Bell lowered the tin cup and smacked his lips. "In the mornin' we'll give him empty guns and take him to the bank with us. That'll be mercy. When the shootin' starts, we'll gutshoot him. If Mase is in sight, Mase can swear he kilt Garrison. Them fools in town will waste time figurin' Garrison is one of us. That'll be justice for a damn' depity who follered us."

"I don't aim to wait that long!" said Windy coldly. "Here's my justice. . . ."

Garrison thought it was a bullet. He wheeled fast and smashed hard knuckles to Windy's sneering mouth and nose. The gun barrel striking at his head swung off wildly as Windy staggered. Garrison jumped to snatch the gun.

He sighted Mase Bragdon, lunging toward him. Mase's

smashing gun barrel dropped him cold to the floor.

IV

Outdoors on the hard, weed-covered ground Garrison's eyes finally opened. Cold stars pinpointed through thinning clouds. He was hog-tied, gagged. When he moved and grunted from pain, a boot kicked his rib.

"Keep quiet. Folks is sleepin'."

Snores drifted out of the nearby brush. Tarp rolls had been brought outside and a guard left against surprise. A horse nickered back of the house where the old corral would be. Garrison closed his eyes and after a little he slept.

He woke with dawn chill clammy on him. Men were moving about in the gray light. He watched Mase Bragdon tramp back to the corral. Tom Bragdon came out of the house with stiff steps and a gun muzzle at his back. The sheriff was standing there before the house when Mase rode his horse from the corral, Whitey Bell and Windy walking beside him.

"You know what to do," said Whitey. "Git goin'."

Mase rode off without looking toward his father. Tom Bragdon stood there, stiffly straight, arms lashed behind with buckskin thongs. He watched Mase out of sight with a gray, haggard look. Then he obeyed the prodding gun and walked silently into the house.

Windy Carter came over. His nose had bled and his upper lip was puffy. He drove a kick savagely to Garrison's side. "I'll gutshoot you in town," he promised thinly.

Two hours later Garrison rode off with them. He'd washed blood off his face, been fed bacon, beans, and coffee. His rifle was in the saddle scabbard, side gun in its holster. Both guns were loaded with empty shells.

Grub was rolled in blankets behind all saddles. They carried nothing else but guns and ammunition. The other guard at the wire gate last night, and the guard posted outside the house all night, were younger men. They'd been rustling with these older renegades like Mase Bragdon had been, Garrison guessed.

The pace was easy toward Talus. Garrison rode thinking of Tom Bragdon, tied and helpless in the old house where, as a young man, he'd faced life with his young wife. Garrison's glance roved to the aging renegades, riding again out of the past, with younger men following their orders. They'd lived too long.

Whitey Bell chortled as they cut across the rough foothills, avoiding the roads. "Makes me feel twenty years younger," he said.

Talus was in sight from a low ridge crest when Whitey pulled up.

"We'll split here, boys. Mex, you and Joe cut over to the west road and ease into town that-away. Curly, you side Windy on the north road. Tie your horses at the side rack of the bank."

Windy cursed with a vicious note. "I aim to keep close to this damn' depity. He's mine."

Whitey said: "There ain't gonna be no gut-shootin' for fun ahead of time, Windy. And you'd do it, you blood-drinkin' old goat."

"Who you callin' names, Whitey? We'll shoot it out right now."

Garrison poised stiffly. But the tall taciturn Red, with the yellow mustache, said: "Curly, you go with Mex and Joe. This ain't no time to tangle with Windy. He's like he used to be. Only worse."

Windy's puffy lip had a wolfish sneer of satisfaction as he stayed close to Garrison.

The three men rode off smartly. Garrison was boxed by the three who were left as they leisurely cut into the north stage road not a mile from town.

It was a blazing morning with a great arc of brassy-blue sky. A six-horse stage whirled out of town. Whitey Bell waved genially. The driver saluted with his whip. Their leisurely progress went by the outer corrals and sheds of town. A button of a kid ran to a yard gate and waved. Whitey waved back.

Since last night Garrison's cold patience had held him passive, like a slaughter-bound sheep. He'd come a long way after this bunch. In Talus, on the main street, he could die to better purpose. Garrison had even nursed a small idea based only on hope. He waited, stony-faced, boxed in by the three gunmen as they advanced at a walk.

The same snag-toothed hostler stood in the yawning doorway of the livery barn and grinned at them. Red's hand answered the hostler. They passed by the Talus *Times* and Garrison sighted the soft red hair of Alma Stevens as she stood inside the counter, talking to two men and a woman. Alma moved to see better through the front windows. She was puzzled, uncertain. Garrison looked away, afraid she might come out and call to him, and so find trouble.

Then they came to the hotel. Garrison glanced up at the windows of the big corner room on the second story. Cracked window shades were pulled half down. Brassy sun glare struck in against a small, shadowy figure peering down at the street. Jimmy Green, still locked in, worried, watchful, who had sighted the yellow-mustached gunman they'd trailed so long

Garrison let out a soft slow breath. This was all he could hope for. They were wheeling in to the bank hitch rack opposite the hotel. Mex Peters and the two younger men loitered on the corner, waiting.

A man came out of the bank and walked away. Whitey Bell spoke under his breath. "Tie your horses. Mex, Red, and me will go in. Stand here at the hitch rack, Windy, with this damn' depity! Curly and Joe stays on the corner there."

Windy watched from the saddle until Garrison stepped down. Whitey Bell and Red waited until Windy was down. Then they walked into the bank. Mex Peters idled in behind them like any other depositor.

Talus had never been more peaceful. A man laughed inside an open doorway nearby. Two bonneted women left a buggy in front of McKay's general store and went inside. The musical clanging of a blacksmith's hammer beat rhythmically through the glass-clear sunlight.

Garrison took perhaps his last look around on earth. Windy stood two steps away, hands poised near the low-slung belt guns. His long, flat nose flared stiffly above grizzled mustache and puffy lip. The wolf-like sneer had never been stronger as he watched the prisoner.

Garrison's sweeping look touched the window where Jimmy Green had been watching. Heart leaped. Breath stopped. His glance cut on down without expression. That window, he saw, was halfway up now. Then suddenly Garrison's stare fixed in cold resentment on the open hotel doorway.

Mase Bragdon's burly figure was swaggering out on the verandah.

"There's your dirty deputy," said Garrison through tight lips.

Windy looked and cursed softly. "Whyn't the fool keep outta sight?" Then death crashed a gunshot inside the bank.

Mase Bragdon ran off the hotel verandah as Garrison jumped at Windy with flesh braced against the smashing slugs Windy would drive into him. He saw Windy's palms slap to the waiting guns.

Whitey Bell was bellowing orders inside the bank. A shot roared from the corner where the younger gunmen stood. And Windy took a queer, lurching step, his hatchet face contorted. A tiny hole had been drilled in Windy's upper vest pocket. Back on his heels, Windy wavered as Garrison flung out a hand and caught one of the guns. It spurted hot powder burns along his wrist. He tried to get the other gun as it swung toward his body. The gun swerved down under his grasp and crashed flame almost against his upper leg. The bullet blow had axe-like force, numbing the leg.

The leg bone was not splintered for it held strongly under the surge of Garrison's desperation. He caught the second gun, too, twisting the muzzle away. His lunge drove Windy back. The first gun came away in the mighty wrench Garrison gave it.

He palmed the heavy steel flatly to Windy's temple with fury that doubled strength. And Windy suddenly was only a sack of flesh, collapsing weakly. Garrison snatched the other gun off the walk cinders where it had dropped, and almost sprawled flat from the bad leg. He staggered over against the brick building front and straightened, with both guns settling hard in perspiring palms.

A bullet ricocheted off the bricks just above his head. Joe had shot at him from the corner. Garrison triggered shots, and Joe ducked to the shelter of the bank corner. Windy was flat on his face. A rifle muzzle thrusting out the second story hotel window hurled its flat report across the street once more. The little San Carlos bookkeeper had drilled Windy and his ledgers were free of doubt.

Garrison swung muzzles toward Mase Bragdon, then held fire. Mase was walking across the street with both guns out. His broad face was grinning. One gun fired, and then the other. Fast hammering shots around the bank corner replied as Mase advanced, still grinning. Mase was shooting at Joe and Curly. Double-crossing his rustling partners.

Garrison had only an instant to think of old Tom Bragdon helplessly waiting. Then Whitey Bell came plunging out of the bank, gun in one hand, heavy canvas sack in the other hand. "You double-crossin' skunk!" he bellowed, opening fire on

Mase. Mex Peters and the tall, lean Red came spilling out at his heels.

Mase had halted in the street dust near the corner, his guns dropping down as lead hit him somewhere. Then his guns swung up again, toward Whitey Bell. Their guns crashed at each other. Garrison shot at the long, lean Red he'd trailed so far.

Red had dropped the canvas sack and made a cat-like spring at sight of Garrison. Trail sign had marked Red as a dead shot. Garrison's bullet hit him. Red's spurting gun muzzle smashed lead along Garrison's side. The trail ended here for one of them.

The triggered gun in Garrison's right hand leaped and roared, and Red folded over, catching at his middle. Garrison reeled, gasping for breath. Mex Peters was down and coming up on a knee, dark face twisting as he brought up a six-gun and fired at Garrison.

He missed. Garrison steadied again with another great effort. His shot drove Mex over backward. Whitey Bell swung around in a lurching run toward his horse, smoking gun in one hand, canvas sack in the other.

Garrison got his breath. "Judgment Day, Whitey!" Both his blasting guns tore lead through the big man's torso. Whitey Bell sprawled down toward Windy's feet. The untied sack spilled gold coins over the walk. Whitey Bell's outreaching, convulsive hand clawed up gold pieces, bright and yellow in the sunlight. He clutched them tightly as he died, rich finally, for a few last seconds.

The gunfire had stopped. Townsmen were fearfully coming out along the walks as Garrison hobbled out through the dust to Mase Bragdon. Mase's shirt was wet with blood, and one arm hung limply. His grin was a crooked effort. Words came thickly.

"Tell the old man they'd have killed us all last night if I hadn't played along. . . ." Mase swallowed hard. "He made a good father and mother. Wish I . . ."

A slim, flying, red-headed figure came to them. Alma went unheedingly to her knees in the street dust. "Mase! Mase!"

"Tom Bragdon's tied up at Mase's old house," Garrison said. "Get out there alone, Alma, and bring him back. Tell him I said Mase can't keep the law in town alone. Tell him I said Mase doesn't know he's out there. I'll swear Mase is lying if he says so."

Alma's greenish-gray eyes held the truth, the hurt, and a great new hope as she looked at Garrison, and then fully into Mase's face.

"The Talus *Times* knows everything," said Alma unsteadily. "But it doesn't print all it knows, Mase, you fiddle-footed fool."

"Mase has settled down," said Garrison, smiling with an effort. "Nice folks, a fine town, pretty girls. Might stay myself."

"Nancy McKay would like that," Alma told him quickly.

"I'm staying, then," said Garrison. His thoughts flashed to the past and the long trail, and settled again here in Talus where the trail had ended. He was smiling a little about the future as the first running men reached them.

ABOUT THE AUTHOR

T. T. Flynn was born Thomas Theodore Flynn, Jr., in Indianapolis, Indiana. He was the author of over a hundred Western stories for such leading pulp magazines as Street & Smith's *Western Story Magazine,* Popular Publications' *Dime Western,* and Dell's *Zane Grey's Western Magazine.* He lived much of his life in New Mexico and spent much of his time on the road, exploring the vast terrain of the American West. His descriptions of the land are always detailed, but he used them not only for local color but also to reflect the heightening of emotional distress among the characters within a story. Following the Second World War, Flynn turned his attention to the book-length Western novel and in this form also produced work that has proven imperishable. Five of these novels first appeared as original paperbacks, most notably *The Man from Laramie* (1954) that was also featured as a serial in *The Saturday Evening Post* and subsequently made into a memorable motion picture directed by Anthony Mann and starring James Stewart. He was highly innovative and inventive and in later novels, such as *Night of the Comanche Moon* (Five Star Westerns, 1995), concentrated on deeper psychological issues as the source for conflict, rather than more elemental motives like greed. Flynn is at his best in stories that combine mystery—not surprisingly, he also wrote detective fiction—with suspense and action in an artful balance. The psychological dimensions of Flynn's Western fiction came increasingly to encompass a confrontation with ethical principles about how one must live, the values that one must hold dear above all else, and his belief that there must be a balance in all things. The cosmic meaning of the mortality of all living creatures had become for him a unifying metaphor for the fragility and dignity of life itself. *The Man from Laramie*, *Night of the Comanche Moon* (1995), *Rawhide* (1996), *Long Journey to Deep Cañon* (1997), *The Devil's Lode* (1999), *Hell's Cañon* (2002), *Reunion at Cottonwood Station* (2003), *Gunsmoke* (2007), and *Last Waltz on Wild Horse* (2008) are among the T.T. Flynn titles available in trade paperback and e-book editions from Amazon Publishing. *Travis* (2011), selected by *Booklist* as one of the Ten Best Westerns published in 2012.